Gruey

Stephen Grucock, alias Gruey, believes:
that even a blob like Wooly can win races; that
Quidsy's brains are in her pigtails; that one day he
will grind Slaphead Nidgey into the dust; and that
anyone with the right attitude can swim through
porridge with wellies on.

His dad believes:
that Gruey was dumped on them by extra-
terrestrials to sabotage the earth.

The extra-terrestrials deny responsibility . . .

Gruey is based on Martin Riley's popular BBC tv
series.

GRUEY

Martin Riley

BBC BOOKS

For all my family and friends, north and south,
with thanks for their ideas and inspiration

Special thanks to Ian Page for starting me off,
Elaine Hill for keeping me on the right track
and Linden Almond for constant support.

Published by BBC Books
a division of BBC Enterprises Ltd
Woodlands, 80 Wood Lane, London, W12 0TT.

First published 1988
©Martin Riley 1988

ISBN 0 563 20641 1

Set in 11/12pt Baskerville by Wilmaset, Birkenhead, Wirral
Printed and bound in England by Richard Clay Ltd, Bungay, Suffolk

CHAPTER ONE

At two minutes and ten seconds past four o'clock, a wave of schoolkids crashed through the main gates of Brudal Road School. A tide of sea-green uniforms flooded the pavement, clogged the bus queues, surged into sweet shops and filled up the road with wheels.

There were track wheels, racing wheels, solid plastic wheels and a pair of rusty spoked wheels – a front one that wobbled a bit, and a back one that made a regular scraping sound as it rubbed against a loose mudguard.

These last two wheels were Stephen Grucock's. They belonged to the clapped-out old pushbike that he was scooting along the kerb, stopping now and then to talk to his mate, Quidsy.

A plaintive voice called out from behind them. "Gruey! Quidsy!" A tall, pale, slightly unfit looking specimen, wearing too many clothes for comfort, was trying to catch up and make a point. It was Peter Woolsmith and he wanted words with Gruey.

Thursday was athletics afternoon, and Gruey had been sounding off in the changing room about how anyone could be good at sport.

"It's all down to having the right attitude. If you got yer attitude right you could jump over Blackpool Tower, you could run faster than Superman's whippet, you could swim through porridge with wellies on!"

Nigel Jackson hadn't agreed, but then Nidgey

didn't agree with anything about Gruey – not even that Gruey had a right to exist. The very sound of Gruey's voice made Nidgey's stomach churn. He fastened him with his narrow-slit eyes. "You don't half talk a load of tripe, Gruey! What use is attitude if you've no talent! I'll tell you what! We'll have a race. We'll pick a runner each, only yours has to be a complete blob with a brilliant attitude. If yours loses you're a mouthy wazzock that knows nowt about sport! If mine loses – I am!"

Gruey had never been known to refuse a challenge. By the end of school he'd picked his "blob". He'd picked Peter Woolsmith without asking him, and now Wooly wanted words. He caught up with Quidsy and Gruey by the traffic lights. "Gruey! I don't want to be in no race!"

Gruey was merciless. "Don't be pathetic! Yer entered!"

Quidsy thought Wooly had a point. "You might have asked him first!"

Quidsia Rahim was good with ideas. Gruey had a theory that the size of her brain was related to the length of her pigtails.

"All right! So I didn't ask him! But he wants to really! . . . You want to be a runner, don't you Wooly? You want to be a champion athlete!"

Wooly was confused at being told so firmly what he wanted. "Yes . . . No . . . Me mam!"

Quidsy gave an exasperated sigh and turned on Gruey. "You know what his mam's like!"

Gruey knew only too well what Wooly's mother was like, and he knew she wasn't going to approve. Gruey was stumped for a moment. He wondered if enough blood was reaching his brain.

6

He pulled off his school tie, stuffed it in his blazer pocket and found new inspiration. "Ninety per cent of people who do the marathon don't get heart attacks!"

"It's not the marathon you've put him in for, is it?" said Quidsy. "It's the five hundred metre suicidal! How's he gonna beat Nigel "slaphead" Jackson?"

"Nidgey!" gasped Wooly, horrified at the prospect.

Gruey tried to calm him down.

"Take it easy. Nidgey's not running. I keep tellin' yer — Nidgey picks a runner to run for him. I pick a runner to run for me."

"Yer not a great picker, are you Gruey?" said Quidsy, observing the agitated Wooly, who was now sweating with exertion and the warm vest his mam made him wear.

"Anyway, me heart's all right. It's me chest!" explained Wooly.

"Sykerlogical!"

Gruey had recently found this word, and was lobbing it about all over the place. Wooly threw it back at him. "You're the one that's sykerlogical!"

"At least I'm not a chicken!" said Gruey, and started squawking and making clucking noises. Some of the people waiting by the lights looked a bit worried, but the green man bleeped and Gruey went scooting off towards Betty's cafe.

Quidsy caught up with him just outside the door. "His mam says he's not to do running!"

Gruey looked at Wooly huffing along the road towards them. "What's that he's doin' now then?"

"That's different!"

"Sykerlogical!"

Wooly arrived, and stood panting outside the cafe. With his vest and shirt and cardigan and jacket and anorak and scarf and hat, it was obvious why he had trouble running.

"Are you all right in there?" asked Quidsy sarcastically. "Do you want to stop at the cafe?"

"I have to! Don't I?" said Wooly bitterly. "It's me home! I live here! Me mam . . ."

Gruey didn't want to hear any more moaning. "You don't know when you're well off!"

"I'm never well off when you're around," said Wooly. "Me mam says you're a bad influence."

Gruey propped his old wreck of a bike against the cafe window. "Yer mam's always havin' a go at me, Wooly. She don't mean it!"

She *did* mean it! Wooly's mam, Betty Woolsmith, was the kind of woman who didn't say what she didn't mean. Betty had coped well with all manner of troubles in her life. She'd had to bring Wooly up on her own and run the cafe as well.

She'd known Gruey too long to be surprised by anything, and just at that moment she was watching him through the cafe window with a look of painful anticipation.

As soon as he was through the door she went for him. "How many times have I told you about leaning that bike against my winder!"

"Four or five times?"

"Four or five hundred!"

"I'll shift it in a minute!"

"You wait till I see your dad!"

"Three Cokes!" said Quidsy, and the bickering stopped while they searched for their cash.

Quidsy dipped into her purse. Gruey dug deep into the lining of his blazer. The great pile of copper that they dumped on the counter did nothing to change Betty's mood. There still wasn't enough till Wooly magicked a 50p piece from his inside pocket.

Gruey watched it vanish into the till. "You should get yours free, Wooly. I mean it's your cafe!"

Betty corrected him. "It's his mother's cafe! Back there in the kitchen it's free. Out here he pays."

As Betty handed Wooly his change, Gruey moved in quick and casual with his regular request. "Lend us 20p for the machine!"

"What's the use? You never win!"

"I will. I've gotta system!"

Wooly gave him the 20p as usual. Gruey stuffed it into the machine. Wooly and Quidsy sat on the table nearby and watched him get slaughtered by Mukron Spacebattlelaserships for the ten billionth time.

"They've speeded it up," he said dolefully as he sat down with the others. "But I'll beat it in the end. It's all a matter of attitude . . . like running!"

Wooly knew what he was driving at. "I can't do this daft race. Me mam'll throw a wobbler!"

"Will she belt yer?" asked Quidsy, sounding more curious than worried.

"No. She'll talk to me. She had me for half an hour yesterday 'cos I went out without me jumper. 'Ner, ner, ner, ner!' I have to look at the wallpaper so I don't go scatty. There's this greasy patch over there by the counter. I'll remember it till the day I die . . ."

Quidsy was fascinated. "What does she say?"

Wooly tried to remember, but all he could see

in his head was the wallpaper pattern. "She says I'm a worry to her."

Gruey grabbed him by the shoulders. "But you won't be after Saturday, will you? She'll be dead proud of you when you've won this race in record time!"

Wooly didn't look convinced. Quidsy neither! "If his mam gets to hear of it he'll never get past the starting line!"

"All right," said Gruey, with devastating logic, "we won't let her find out."

Quidsy thought that would be difficult! "She's better'un Superwoman. She can see him doing wrong through brick walls, and then she'll want to know who put him up to it, which is dead obvious, and yer mam'll know in point nought one of a second, and yer dad'll knock seven bells out of yer, and yer won't be able to say I didn't tell yer!"

A voice came from behind. "And if you try coppin' out of this, I'll knock so many bells out of you you'll never ring again."

It was the dreaded Nigel Jackson! The way they went on about Nidgey anyone would think he was a ten-foot-high muscle-bound mixture of Jaws, Mr T. and Frankenstein's monster, whereas in actual fact he was only five foot three and a half with his Martens air-soles under him. While Quidsy was giving Gruey the benefit of her advice, he'd slipped through the cafe door unnoticed. Now he was standing right behind Gruey, gripping the back of his neck.

Gruey tried to ignore the pain. "Y'all right, Nidgey?" said Gruey, making out that he didn't care about having both the karate death spots in his neck squeezed at once.

"I'm all right," said Nidgey, releasing his grip, "but you won't be if you don't turn up on Saturday. I've heard you've been having trouble persuading some poor mug to run for you?"

Nidgey looked at Quidsy, who looked straight back at him, and then at Wooly who smiled uncomfortably.

"Him?" said Nidgey contemptuously.

"Mebbee," said Gruey.

"What are you gonna do? Put a rocket up him?"

Gruey squared up to Nidgey. "Attitude. It's all a matter of the right attitude!"

Quidsy joined in on Gruey's side. "An' training. That's important too!"

Nidgey looked at Wooly and laughed. "You'd be better off melting him down for scrap!"

"All right, smartypants!" said Quidsy. "Who's running for you? Billy Whizz?"

"Never you mind!" scoffed Nidgey, tapping his nose with his finger. "See you over the waste ground Saturday afternoon! Be there or be squashed!"

Pleased with his own wit, Nidgey made a cool exit from the cafe. He stopped outside to smirk through the window and then gave Gruey's poor old bike just enough of a tilt to send it clattering down onto the pavement.

Betty heard the sound of nearly breaking glass and screamed at Gruey. "Shift that bike!"

Nidgey whistled as he walked away. Wooly sipped his Coke and contemplated his fate. "How am I gonna get out of this one?"

When Gruey returned from propping the bike up against a different part of the window, Wooly had made up his mind. "Tell Nidgey you were wrong. Tell him you made a mistake!"

Gruey wasn't struck on this idea. "Mistake! There's no mistake! . . . I've got a plan!"

Quidsy and Wooly made noises as though they were going to be sick.

"A plan!" insisted Gruey. "Who was it saved us from the alley-gang with me pellet-firing cannon?"

"Nearly blew us to bits!" said Quidsy.

"What about the peddle-powered atomic canal boat?"

"Nearly drowned us!" said Wooly.

Gruey exploded with indignation. "You're always findin' fault, you two! Where's your team spirit? Where's yer will to win?"

As he made this stirring appeal, Gruey became more and more excited. He climbed onto his chair to address the multitude of two. "Courage! Determination! Victory to Wooly!"

He climbed onto the table and raised his voice another ten decibels. "The power of positive planning!"

Betty wasn't impressed. "Will you get off that table, get out of my cafe and take that bloomin' boneshaker off my winder!"

Betty's sudden outburst so shocked Gruey that he stepped backwards, let rip a yell of fright as he lost his balance, kicked an ashtray into the cake display and then crashed over like King Kong at the end of the film. Chairs and crockery shot off in different directions.

When the dust had settled, Gruey lay moaning among the wreckage. Quidsy and Wooly picked him up and muttered sorrowful apologies as they escorted him out of the door. Betty watched them through the window and saw the guilt turn into laughter as soon as they were out of reach.

"Kids!" she muttered to herself.

"Kids!" said Mr Grucock later in the evening, as he watched Gruey trying to balance a cork and two forks on top of a milk bottle – like he'd seen once in a science book!

Gruey was shaping his plan to turn Wooly into a mega sports-hero. There was something he needed to borrow from his dad, but it was hard to find the right moment to ask. The enquiry into how come Gruey was so battered and bruised had been going on for some time.

"Why don't you tell us the truth?" said Mrs Grucock.

Gruey told her. "I fell off the table, honest!"

This wasn't enough for Mr Grucock. "What were you *doing* on the table?"

"Making a point!"

"Do you know what it's like trying to get sense out of you? It's like having a close encounter with an alien life form! I bet you're a Venusian that got dumped in our carrycot to sabotage the earth."

Gruey liked that idea. "Hey, d'y'think so? Perhaps I'm an extra-terrestrial intelligence wi' secret superpowers who's lost his memory."

"Lost his marbles, more like!" groused his dad.

Mrs Grucock took another look at her son's bruises and had an inspiration. "Has that Nigel Jackson been picking on you again? You wait till I see his mother!"

This suggestion didn't please Gruey. He leapt up out of his chair in horror! "No! Not that! It was an accident – honest!"

Somehow Gruey bashed the table. Somehow the milk bottle he'd been playing with, the forks in the cork, and one or two completely innocent items went flying.

Mr Grucock was convinced. "All right! I believe you! Yer a living breathing accident. What were you doin' with that milk bottle?"

"It were an experiment . . . for science! Can I borrow yer watch, dad?"

"You had one for your birthday!"

"It's bust!"

"Surprise, surprise!"

"It's for science."

"Yer not balancing my watch on no milk bottle!"

"We've got the day off tomorrow, an' I've got to time things for me homework!"

This was the kind of old rubbish that parents hear all the time, but it did the trick. Gruey's dad didn't want to stand in the way of his son's education, and if Gruey had a day off it was better he was kept busy. There was one condition. "If this watch don't come back to me in one perfect piece, I'll put you in a big black plastic bag, drop you in the canal and time how long it takes you to drown!"

"Why do adults always gripe on!" thought Gruey.

Later that night he lay in bed and tried to puzzle out a Grueyistic theory to explain parental whingeing. "Maybe their brain cells deteriorate as they get older. They can't communicate with my generation. I'm like an alien life form to them."

After a while Gruey lost his grip on these deep thoughts and drifted off.

He slept, and dreamed his dreams.

He dreamt in Full Colour Cinemascope with Quadrophonic Sound.

He dreamt of triumphing over Nidgey, with all the school cheering him on.

He dreamt of Wooly winning the race and Gruey's training method becoming world famous.

He dreamt he was a Venusian, and had to leap out of bed in the morning to check if he'd turned green.

Gruey was a great dreamer!

Once he was out of bed and half into his clothes, he started burrowing around the room. Gruey's bedroom was a tip. There were piles of comics, and half-finished models, drawings, plans, lego things, bits of machinery, books, posters, socks, trainers, sports kit and bike parts, but Gruey knew exactly where everything was . . . more or less.

After a few minutes he found a not very flattering drawing of Nidgey with "The Enemy" written underneath. He pinned it to the wall, pulled out an old chest expander with one spring missing and started to do his morning exercises. "I'll show you, Nidgey! Wooly's gonna win that race tomorrow! And one day . . . I'm gonna grind you into pulp!"

Gruey gave a scream as he lost his grip on the chest expander and nearly caught his belly button in its springs.

His mam called to him from downstairs. "Gruey! What are you doing up there?"

"Just me exercises!" shouted Gruey, as he performed a series of Kung Fu moves against the wardrobe.

Mrs Grucock shouted out what she would do if he didn't come straight down the stairs. Seconds later Gruey stumbled into the kitchen.

"Where's me dad?"

"Gone to work, for a bit of peace."

"Has he left his watch?"

His mam handed him the precious device, with a dire warning. "Just you look after it! You know what he's like!"

Gruey knew. He knew why, too. "It's his brain cells. He's deteriorating!"

"So am I!" said his mam. "And for the same reason!"

This remark was wasted on Gruey, who ignored his breakfast and went rooting through the cupboard for his balaclava. It was an important part of "the plan".

His mam was a bit mystified, since the sun was shining bright and warm through the kitchen window.

"It's for an experiment!" said Gruey. Out came old jigsaws, old jumpers, old jamjars, gloves, glass cases, a pile of old Sunday supplements, and finally . . . "I've got it!"

"I'm so pleased," said his mam, who wasn't. "Eat yer breakfast!"

"No time now! See yer!"

The back door banged. Mrs Grucock sat down and started eating Gruey's cornflakes. Gruey raced on his way to see Wooly with his balaclava, and his Gruey-type plan buzzing in his brain.

He took the short cut across the waste ground.

Various bits of ruined house had been left standing, and one particular old bit of wall was very special to Gruey. He couldn't walk past without stopping to look.

Gruey looked at the Wall. The Wall looked back at Gruey. It challenged him. It dared him. It mocked him. It looked as though you could jump it with a good run-up, but Gruey had tried and failed a dozen times. He stood by it. He looked over it at the boggy mud patch which never dried, even in high summer. He brushed a few pebbles off the top bricks – as if that would make any difference! He walked away, counting his paces. He turned and crouched ready to run.

"Get on with it, then!" It was Quidsy. "Get on with it!"

"How can I? You've ruined me concentration!"

"I can do it!"

"So can I! It's all a matter of attitude!"

"Let's see you, then!"

Gruey was trapped and he knew it!

He unstrapped his dad's watch and gave it to Quidsy. "You'd better look after this," he said, as though he was making his last will and testament.

Then he took a deep breath, and started to run.

As Gruey reached the Wall and took off into the air, a look of exhilaration appeared on his face. A thought of triumph flashed through his mind like an inter-city special.

"I'm gonna make it!!"

CHAPTER TWO

While Gruey was in mid-air, Wooly was in a deep trance. He was sitting in the cafe, meditating on the grease stain by the counter, while his mother's voice went in one ear and out the other.

"And what would have happened if I hadn't found out, that's what I want to know! Running daft races with a chest like yours! I can't be looking out for you all the time! . . . Peter! Peter, are you listening to me?"

Betty flapped a hand in front of Wooly's face and brought him back to the land of the living.

"What's going on?"

Wooly was as dozy as a Care Bear with dead batteries. Betty assumed, as always, that he must be sickening for something. "It's no good, Peter! I'm gonna have to take you to the doctor's to have your ears syringed."

Wooly could hear that perfectly, and he didn't like the sound of it. Luckily medical matters were put off by Quidsy and Gruey banging on the cafe door.

"Here they are," said Betty wrathfully as she marched down to let them in. "Mr Mischief and the Queen of Crime!"

The bunch of keys jangled, the door opened, and in staggered Gruey, plastered with muck. His inter-city thought of triumph had been seriously delayed.

Quidsy was trying not to giggle. "He's had an accident."

"I can see that, Quidsia," said Betty with a despairing sigh.

"But his dad's watch is all right." Quidsy dangled the proof before her, but it didn't bring Betty any joy.

"So I see. It's his poor mother's heart he's broken! . . . You're daft, the pair of you, only he's the daftest. Get out the back, Gruey, and clean yerself up!"

Gruey sloped off for a wash, and Betty turned on Quidsy. "Now listen here, 'laffing girl' – Peter's told me all about this ridiculous race tomorrow, and I'm not allowing it. Peter's not a well boy, you know!"

"Gruey says it's all sykerlogical!"

"Gruey reads too many books!"

Wooly had been ignored long enough to edge his way almost to the door before his mam spotted him. "Peter!"

"Can I go out now, mam?"

"No races!" pronounced Betty. "And I'll be looking out to make sure!"

As she gave this warning there was a terrible crash from behind her back. Gruey appeared, clean but wet, with a bit of patterned pottery in his hand. "I got soap in me eyes and I couldn't see to find the towel . . . I think I've got this alien power to attract disaster."

Betty flung open the door. "Well for crying out loud, go and attract it somewhere else!"

Half an hour later, as Gruey, Quidsy and Wooly sat on the Grucock back step trying to ignore the smell from the drains, Gruey found out why

Wooly was wearing a face like a blancmange in a heat wave. He couldn't believe it.

"He *told* her? He told her about the race???"

"She hypnotises me!" explained Wooly. "Me mam . . ."

Quidsy interrupted. "Me mam, me mam, me mam! That's all we ever hear from you!"

"But me mam's keeping a look-out! The race is off!"

Gruey wasn't beaten. "She won't know it's you!"

"Don't be daft! She'll recognise me!"

Gruey turned to Quidsy. "Give us that safety pin."

It was all part of the plan. Quidsy produced a large nappy pin. Gruey produced a shapeless piece of knitwear from his pocket. Next minute the reluctant Wooly was sitting with a balaclava pulled down over his head and fastened across his nose. You could see just enough of him to know how irritated he was. "Get it off! I can't run in this! It prickles, an' I bet I look a right wazzock!"

He did.

"You'll get used to it," said Quidsy in a tone of voice she'd picked up from lying adults. "We'll train you in it. You'll be a mystery runner! The man in the knitted mask! You'll be famous!"

Wooly didn't share Quidsy's romantic view of the future. "I'm not somebody out of the *Beano* annual. Me mam'll lock me in the cafe and talk to me serious for hours."

"Don't be a wet wally!" said Gruey.

Quidsy tried a more encouraging tone. "Go on! It'll be a laugh!"

"For you, yeah!" Wooly wasn't encouraged.

Quidsy was exasperated. "Go home then. Tell yer mam to change yer nappy."

That did it. Wooly had to choose between looking a wally and being a wimp. It wasn't much of a choice.

"Right then!"

"You're a hero, Wooly!" said Quidsy, and then pulled out a notebook. "Training part one – diet!"

Gruey pulled out the *Ladybird Book of Athletic Training*.

"Protein. That's what it says here!"

Quidsy swung her pigtails over her shoulders. "Time I went home for a visit!"

Quidsy hadn't been home all morning and her dad had found it quiet enough to think about income tax and V.A.T. and all the miseries and troubles of trying to run a cornershop. He wasn't enjoying himself. "Where's our Quidsia? I prefer the headache I get from her yelling the place down to the headache I get from worrying!"

Mrs Rahim looked up from stacking the vegetable rack. "She's off with that Stephen Grucock."

Gruey was another one of Mr Rahim's headaches. "Why do you think she's so fond of him?"

"Same reason she was fond of that one-eyed rabbit we had – the one that used to bite through its cage and pick fights with the cat!"

While Mr Rahim was weighing up the possible similarity between Gruey and a one-eyed rabbit, he was suddenly confronted with a masked face peering through the window.

His wife grabbed him by the arm. ". . . Quick! Behind the counter! Phone the police!"

Mr Rahim dived for cover. Just for a moment

he thought he'd better take a long holiday – just for a moment. And then he realised he'd been taken for a ride already, as Wooly, Quidsy and Gruey clanged through the shop door.

Mrs Rahim carried on the pretence. "Too late! They've got us cornered!"

Quidsy was puzzled at the sight of her parents crouched down behind the counter. "Mam? . . . Dad?"

"Don't argue with her. Do what she says!" gasped Mrs Rahim in mock terror.

If there was one thing Quidsy didn't like, it was adults acting silly. She decided to ignore their play-acting and ask what she'd come to ask. "Have you still got them dented cans I cleared off the shelves yesterday?"

Mr Rahim's curiosity brought him back to reality. "Dented cans?"

"Protein!" said Gruey. "Wooly needs a load of it quick!"

Quidsy's mam wasn't satisfied. "Why? And why is he wearing a balaclava when it's roasting hot out there?"

Quidsy started to give what promised to be a long explanation, but her dad cut her short. "We're better off not knowing! . . . You want dented cans?"

"Yeah."

"Fine. Take the box and take Stephen Grucock and the Masked Avenger out of our shop!"

"It's the lead in the petrol," said Mrs Rahim, as she watched the kids racing down the street. "It makes them hyperactive!"

Over at the waste ground, inside what looked like a half-demolished shed, Wooly sat with a spoon, a dented tin of cold beans, and very little enthusiasm.

Gruey was trying to liven him up. " 'Masked Avenger'. That'll be your pro running name. We'll tour round the world . . . make a fortune."

"Twenty-five per cent for your manager!" said Quidsy, making a note in her exercise book.

"And yer trainer!" said Gruey.

Quidsy was enjoying the fantasy. "All over the world your fans'll be running about in balaclavas."

Wooly didn't seem convinced. He swallowed the last spoonful of baked beans in tomato sauce as though they were boiled slugs in pondslime.

Gruey checked his dad's watch. "One tin in four minutes fifty seconds. Hardly a world record!"

Wooly burped. "It is if you hate beans!"

"They'll give you energy!" said Quidsy.

"What for?" asked Wooly, nervously.

Quidsy was on her feet and ready to go. She handed Wooly his headgear. "Circuit training!" she announced.

There wasn't a gym handy, and there wasn't any sports equipment going spare, but Quidsy and Gruey weren't short of invention. After an hour of half-brick weight training, French skipping for stamina, and running up and down the stairs for endurance, Gruey and Quidsy sent Wooly off on the back-yard hurdles.

Whether it was beans or new-found confidence, the Masked Avenger was doing really well over the garden fences.

It was a pity that he fell on the last.

It was a pity that it was Nidgey's back fence.

And it was an even greater pity that Nidgey was sat on the other side, just below Wooly as he fell.

There were shouts of unseen pain and anger. Quidsy and Gruey ran over to see what the matter was. As they arrived, the red-faced and ferocious Nidgey rose into view. Even if he didn't block out the light from the sun, the effect was the same. It hadn't taken him long to realise it wasn't the S.A.S. on parachute training.

"Yer a wazzock, Gruey!"

Next to appear from behind the fence was a tall girl in a tracksuit, who had enough strength to haul up the dazed Wooly with one hand. When she'd got him on his feet she pulled up the balaclava from where it had slipped over his eyes, and asked a reasonable enough question. "What are you tryin' to prove? What's with this blind kamikaze fence hoppin'?"

"He's training," said Quidsy. "He's a mystery runner!"

"It's Peter Woolsmith!" shouted the exasperated Nidgey. "The whole world knows it's Peter Woolsmith!"

"Not his mam," said Quidsy. "She don't know!"

While Nidgey's mind boggled at this, Gruey looked unhappily at the girl in the tracksuit. "Yer not running for Nidgey, are you?"

Nidgey interrupted before she had a chance to answer. "Never you mind! Tomorrow afternoon *your* mystery runner is gonna get run into the ground by *my* mystery runner ... no matter how many garden walls he jumps over. Now buzz off out of it!"

Gruey buzzed off out of it. They tried a few more protein-filled beanfeasts on Wooly but he didn't want any more beans or anything else. He took off the balaclava and walked despondently back to the cafe. Gruey and Quidsy tried to talk him round, but Wooly had good reason for abandoning hope.

"Don't you know who that was with Nidgey? . . . It was Annie Mapin! She's the best runner in the school! What's the point?"

The odds were stacking up against them, but Gruey wasn't one to admit defeat. "We've got to stick to the schedule! You've got to apply yerself! It's all a matter of havin' the right attitude!"

No amount of facts could stand in the way of a Gruey theory in full flight, but Wooly didn't seem as convinced as he should have been. Nor was he made any happier when his mam emerged from the cafe and dragged him in for his dinner. He was still full from his earlier beanfeast, but he couldn't explain, not without giving the game away.

After Gruey and Quidsy had reported home, and had their own pit stop refills, they met up at the waste ground to wait for Wooly's return. The Wall was as challenging as ever, and Quidsy was too. "Go on then! Have another go at it!"

"I can jump it. I know I can. It's all attitude, same as with Wooly's running."

"What happened last time then?"

"It was the wind."

"It's not windy now."

It looked like Gruey was up for the high jump

again, but Wooly arrived and saved him from more bruising. "Where have you been?" said Gruey, quickly diverting attention away from his wall-jumping problem.

Wooly sat down and gave an almighty belch. "I've been having me dinner, haven't I? Me mam thought I looked a bit peaky, so she gave me loads. I had to eat it all in case she suspected summat, and it were sausage and beans . . . loads and loadsa beans!"

"They'll help you run," said Quidsy brightly.

"They did!" moaned Wooly. "I've been back and forwards to the lav so many times me mam thought I must have some sort of stomach bug, and now I'm fulla that medicine that tastes like chalk and cement mix!"

Quidsy consulted her pigtails. "Kaoline and morphine. That's no good for your training!"

Wooly pulled a plastic carrier bag out of his pocket. "I'm not doing any this afternoon. Me mam says I have to go for the shopping!"

"That's all right," said Gruey optimistically.

Wooly's face dropped as he realised what might be coming. "No. It's *not* all right!"

"Yes it is!" said Gruey.

The people in the bus queue were either amused, annoyed or pretended that it wasn't happening. They weren't normally treated to the sight of a young lad in a tracksuit with a balaclava on his head, doing star jumps and press-ups while they waited for the number fifty-six to town. Wooly had the feeling that he was being stared at . . . and he was right.

By the time the bus arrived, Wooly had worked up quite a sweat and his face was itching under the balaclava. Gruey and Quidsy steadfastly refused to let him take it off, even after the bus driver made some sarky comments about under-age hijackers, and a cheeky girl had asked if he was a famous person trying not to be recognised or just covering up his spots.

"Do I *have* to wear this thing?"

Quidsy spelled it out for him again. "You've got to run in it in case yer mam's about, and if you've got to run in it you've got to train in it."

"I'm not training! I'm shopping!"

"Yer training *and* shopping!"

The "Simultaneous Activity Shop and Train Technique" invented by Quidsy and Gruey meant Wooly had to dash at maximum speed, in his balaclava and tracksuit, up and down the aisles of the supermarket, pausing only to pick up items on his mam's list, while Gruey timed him.

"He was three minutes fifteen seconds on Cheese Counter Corner, and three thirty-five in Biscuit Bend! . . . Where is he now?"

Quidsy peered over the top of the shelves. "Here he comes – round by the frozen meat!"

Gruey consulted the precious timepiece. "Four minutes forty! Me gran could do better! Have you got the tea ready?"

Wooly came skidding to a halt with the trolley and Quidsy threw in the Purple Label Extra Strong Breakfast Special Wonderbags. (Now with even more perforations.)

Wooly collapsed over the trolley handles.

Quidsy shoved the list before his tired eyes. "Don't stop now! Half a pound of bacon!"

"I've been that way . . ." panted Wooly.

Gruey pressed the lap-timer-facility and gave him a helping shove towards the meat counter. "Go!"

Wooly went – at high speed – just as two other trolleys moved more sedately towards the same spot. Quidsy and Gruey saw the danger and shouted both together.

"LOOK OUT!"

It was too late. With a crunch of metal, a cracking of glass, a bouncing of plastic bottles, a flowing of milk, an oozing of honey and a rolling of tins, tomatoes and French Golden Delicious . . . the supermarket experienced its first shopping trolley pile-up.

Quidsy and Gruey ran to pull Wooly out of the wreckage. The other victims were also picking themselves up off the floor and thinking of bloody revenge.

Wooly didn't like the looks they were giving him, or the look on the manager's face as he strode towards them like Wyatt Earp down Dodge City High Street.

Wooly bolted for the exit. Quidsy and Gruey backed off slowly from the collection of murderous looks and then bolted after him.

After that fiasco Quidsy suggested that they try the "Single Activity Shop and Train Technique". This involved the revolutionary idea of doing one thing at a time.

Wooly insisted on doing his mam's shopping

first, and that meant trailing across town to find another supermarket – one where they weren't on the wanted list!

When that was done they headed back through the openair precinct in the centre of town. Quidsy sat on the side of the ornamental pool. "I'm whacked!"

Gruey slumped beside her. "An' me!"

"Me too!" said Wooly, but Gruey had other ideas.

"Not yet. You've got an ideal opportunity here. Three times round the precinct is about five hundred metres. Get going!"

Wooly didn't look like he was going anywhere. Quidsy had an inspiration. "If you do a good time we'll cancel the protein input. No more beans!"

The thought of this set him off at full pelt . . . and then something extraordinary happened. As usual on a Saturday, there were quite a few people in the precinct and, as was also usual, they were mostly bored. The sight of Wooly racing round the square in his balaclava was a welcome distraction.

"It must be some sort of charity stunt."

"Is it a sponsored funny run or summat?!"

"It's the Masked Avenger in training," said Gruey.

That did it!

"Come on the Masked Avenger!"

"Go for a gold!"

"Here he goes. Here he goes. Here he goes!"

Soon there were shouts from all over the precinct. Wooly had a supporters club! It could have made him stop there and then and creep away in embarrassment, but it didn't. It worked a kind of Wembley magic. It lifted him. It changed him into a new Wooly.

There wasn't unqualified enthusiasm. One or two policemen consulted their radios and adopted an "about to take action" attitude.

But Wooly was in the home straight now, racing towards Gruey, who stood with his dad's watch gripped in his hand. "Come on, Avenger! Sprint finish!"

Wooly gave Gruey what he was shouting for, and tore into the last hundred yards. A dozy kid was bent over in front of the pool.

"GERROUTOFTHEWAY!!!!" screamed Quidsy.

The dozy kid got out of the way. Unfortunately he was a dozy skateboarder and he left his means of transport behind him. Next second Wooly was "flying" on one leg towards Gruey, who fell backwards on impact into one of the few precinct ornamental pools in England still supplied with water.

Wooly fell down exhausted. The crowd roared approval and then clicked back into their Saturday Pursuits programs. Gruey squelched out of the pool, dripping horribly polluted water – the watch still tightly grasped. "Wooly! Yer brilliant! A world record beater!"

"No more beans! You said!"

"No more beans!" said Quidsy. "What was his time, Gruey?"

Gruey consulted the watch. After he'd glanced at it, he stared at it. Then he squinted at it. Then he held it to his ear. Then he shook it and listened again. "Oh no!" he groaned. "It's stopped!"

Wooly and Quidsy were waiting outside when Gruey finally emerged from the jewellers.

"How much?" asked Quidsy.

"Five quid," answered Gruey in a flat, off-hand "end of the world but I'm not bothered" voice. "Pay when I pick it up tomorrow."

Wooly was flabbergasted at Gruey's cool. "Five quid! You've not got five quid!"

"I *will* have! You've got to be positive!"

"Oh yeah," said Quidsy. "How are you gonna explain it to yer dad?"

"I'll manage," said Gruey.

It was an easy thing for Gruey to say, but he didn't seem to be managing that well, when he faced a barrage of fatherly aggravation over the kitchen table.

"Let me get this right, Star Fleet Commander. Just by chance you happened to notice with your extrasensory powers that my chromatic, diatronic, easy-action digital wristwatch was out of synch with the atomic clock at Greenwich."

"It weren't working right. It weren't my fault."

"And because you had the idea of doing summat nice for me, in advance of next Father's Day, you put it in to be repaired."

"Yeah."

"Knowing full well that they charge five quid just for spitting on the glass and wiping it with a rag!"

By now his dad's temperature was well over boiling point and Gruey was fighting as hard as any doctor to bring it back down. "I'll pay for it."

"Too flippin' right, Mr Experiment!" shouted

Mr Grucock. "An' it'll be back on my wrist tomorrow night or you'll pay for it in ways you never imagined – even in that black hole you call a mind."

Gruey realised there was to be no cooling him down. "You're upset aren't you, dad?"

His father snarled at him through clenched teeth. "Get . . . my . . . watch . . . back!!!"

Gruey lay in bed and thought how unreasonable it was for his dad to get so upset over petty problems when he had the final showdown with Nidgey looming tomorrow. Never mind watches. There was honour at stake.

That night he had one of his wide-screen surround-sound dreamaramas which featured Mr Grucock as Darth Vader and Gruey as Star Fleet Commander.

Dad-Vader was threatening him with a Deadly-spacelasergun and demanding the return of his "Time Machine" while Wooly, as Super-Space-Hero Lightning Boy Woolsmith, was speeding to get help.

Unfortunately Wooly didn't make it back in time with the space-cavalry and Gruey was getting badly zapped until his faithful old alarm clock cut in to save him from certain death.

Gruey lay in bed for a moment recovering from his dreamtime dust-up. Just when he'd got over his nightmare, real life hit him smack in the face. He grimaced at the drawing of Nidgey the Enemy, still pinned to the wall.

"Today's the day, Nidgey! The Big Race!"

And then something else flashed through

Gruey's mind, something connected with the race and just as important.

In a matter of minutes Gruey was hobbling through the kitchen, one battered boot in place, the other half on, trainers, shorts, and other items of sports gear tucked under his arm.

"Eat yer breakfast," said his mam.

"No time!" said Gruey.

"There he is!" said Quidsy. She'd been waiting in the cafe with Wooly all morning and Gruey had only just arrived. "Where have you been? He's losin' his bottle."

"It's me mam!" said Wooly. "She's watchin' me like a hawk! She says she's goin' over the waste ground when the race is on to make sure it's not me running."

Gruey couldn't see any cause for concern. "You'll be wearing my running gear. You'll have my balaclava on! How's she gonna tell?"

"She just will!" Wooly let out a surprise burp. "An' I don't think all them beans were a good idea!" (Burp.) "I still feel as if I'm going to be sick."

"Think positive!" said Gruey. "You can and you will!"

"I hope not," said Wooly, clutching his stomach.

Gruey glanced at his dad's watch. "You've only got to equal the time you did in the precinct, and you'll win!"

Quidsy was amazed, but not at Wooly's running. "You got the watch back!"

"That's why I'm late," explained Gruey. "I've been around a few of the kids to tell them about

33

the race. Y'see, they all think Wooly's hopeless, so they were happy to put a bet on it. I made 'em give me their money first, and I said I'd give 'em back double if Wooly weren't first past the tape this afternoon."

Wooly looked even more sick. Gruey continued blithely. "Then I spent the money getting me dad's watch out of the menders. It cost me a fortune!"

"Oh brilliant!" cut in Quidsy. "What if he loses? They'll all be after you for their money. Then what?"

Gruey sighed philosophically. "At least I won't be in the canal in a plastic bag . . . And anyway, you won't lose will you, Wooly? Just imagine them shoppers behind you in the supermarket. Just imagine the crowd in the precinct cheering you on . . ."

"Nidgey!" whispered Quidsy.

"Yeah!" said Gruey. "Just imagine Nidgey behind you!"

"It's *you* I'm behind!" said Nidgey, who was indeed! He leaned over and dropped a bank note with the Duke of Wellington's picture on it in front of Gruey. "I hear you've been goin' round takin' bets. Well this here says Mystery Man Wooly hasn't got the slightest chance of winning . . . and that means you owe me a tenner if I'm right! – Right?"

"Right," said Gruey, smiling nervously.

The Duke of Wellington didn't seem to be smiling. Nidgey wasn't either. "And I want paying straight after the race! Straight after! . . . And don't be late!"

Out marched Nidgey, and in walked a foreboding silence.

After a while Quidsy gave Wooly a squeeze round the shoulders. "You've got to win now, or it's goodbye Gruey!"

CHAPTER THREE

Quidsy wasn't the only person who was worried. Gruey's mam had noticed that he'd failed to arrive for his midday feed, and started to worry about the watch. It didn't take her long to walk round to the Rahims' shop and make enquiries.

"Yes!" said Mrs Rahim. "He came in earlier looking for Quidsy, and he *was* wearing an expensive watch. Is it a present?"

"It's a liability! If it's not back in one piece tonight, there'll be murder done in our house! I'd better go and hunt for him."

"If there's trouble brewing, Quidsy'll be there too. I'll come and help you. I expect they'll be in one of the usual places?"

"Cafe, canal, old bridge . . ."

" . . . building site, waste ground!"

Mr Rahim was left to serve the customers while the two women set out on their walkabout.

A crowd of spectators had gathered at the waste ground, many of them with a financial interest in the big race.

Wooly was doing a kind of limbering up, which consisted in waving his arms about as though he was swimming a dry-land butterfly stroke, and glancing round to see if his mam had arrived. Gruey's running gear didn't fit him very well, and the balaclava was itching again. He felt silly.

Quidsy was trying to get him to relax, which was

impossible. Nidgey was edgy too. He kept pacing up and down and looking at his watch, and looking at Annie Mapin, who seemed completely at her ease. She hadn't changed into any stylish running gear. She was sitting on an upturned milk crate, watching Wooly's antics with amusement.

Gruey and Nidgey looked at their watches both together, and nodded.

"Right!" said Nidgey. "We need two to hold the tape."

While two willing punters sorted out the finishing line, Nidgey strolled over to Annie. "Yer not botherin' wi' running gear then? Not worth the effort, is it?"

Annie smiled up at him. "No. I'm not bothering at all!"

"Eh?"

"I'm not running!"

Nidgey's mouth dropped open. His ears went red. "You told me . . ."

"I didn't tell you a thing, Nigel Jackson! I said I'd see . . . and I've seen! I'm not runnin'!"

She made sure everybody could hear the last three words. Nidgey's face went the same colour as his ears. He moved closer and hissed in Annie's ear. "You can't let me down now!"

Annie stood up. By now she had everybody's complete attention. "For one thing, this isn't a proper track. I've got a race on next week and I can't afford a stupid accident. *Plus* . . . You throw your weight about too much, Nidgey! Run yer own race!"

All the faces turned to Nidgey, who was now the colour of a pickled beetroot. He was trapped.

37

"I will then! I've done no training, but I'll only have to walk fast to beat the Balaclava Blob . . . An' then we'll have some paying out to do, won't we Gruey?"

The faces turned to Gruey. He kicked a stone, looked at an imaginary bird flying past and said as coolly as possible under the circumstances: "Let's get on with it!"

Wooly and Nidgey walked across the waste ground to the starting line. Annie Mapin was chosen to give them the signal, which didn't please Nidgey who felt betrayed and set up.

But he also felt confident of winning. All that "attitude" stuff of Gruey's was hogwash. Wooly was a blob, and blobs didn't win races. And then there was the pleasure of proving Gruey to be the wazzock that he was, and the pleasure of taking money off him afterwards. The blush disappeared from Nidgey's ears. All his thoughts became happy ones.

Not so for Wooly. The thought passing through *his* head as they turned to face the distant finishing line was, "Oh, no!"

It wasn't because he was a poor blob who felt he was about to lose a race. It was because he was a poor blob who'd just seen his mother arrive when he was hoping she wasn't coming.

Betty marched straight up to Gruey. "Now then Stephen Grucock! Where's my Peter? I've been looking round for him everywhere!"

"I dunno!"

"I've told you! No running!"

"I know. I know . . . He's had to go . . ." (the blood supply to his brain failed again) ". . . off!"

Quidsy dived in quickly, trying to generate an

idea by twirling her pigtails. "He's er . . . er . . . not very well!"

Betty believed it. "I'm not surprised. He kept clutching his stomach last night and moaning summat about beans."

Gruey winked and gave Quidsy a secret thumbs-up sign for first-class fibbing under difficult conditions. Then a voice in his ear sent his chirpiness into a nose-dive. "Got you!"

It was his mam – and Quidsy's mam with her. They'd come to the end of their walkabout and found the lost tribe. Mrs Grucock weighed up the scene before her and decided that there was potential trouble somewhere, and that Gruey was bound to be in the middle of it.

"Listen to me, my son. I don't know what you're plotting in that addled brain of yours, but whatever it is you'd better unplot it fast!"

It was too late for that. Annie Mapin's hanky dropped, and the two runners leapt off their marks like Olympic champions.

Gruey forgot everything in his excitement. "They're off! They're off!"

All attention switched to the race. It was unbelievable. Wooly was in the lead. He was well in the lead!

Betty gazed into the distance. "Why's that lad runnin' in a balaclava?"

Gruey didn't answer her. He was too busy leaping up and down, shouting himself hoarse, willing Wooly to win! "Come on the Masked Avenger!"

Wooly had gone into the other world. He was the other Wooly that won races, the Masked Avenger that the crowd had cheered round the precinct. He didn't need to think about running. It was as though his legs were doing it all *for* him.

The trouble was it left his brain free, and his brain was fretting about how his mam was standing staring at him, right by the finishing line. The Masked Avenger carried on running, but Wooly's brain got into a panic and started sending "slow down" messages to his legs.

Gruey saw him pull back. "Don't stop! You can do it! Think positive! . . . Look out! – He's gaining on you!"

Betty was more interested in the Masked Avenger's legs than his speed. "It's his knees. That's what it is! I know them knees from somewhere!"

Nidgey was pounding after Wooly, sweating and straining and gulping the air down. He didn't care if it hurt. He didn't care if all his blood vessels burst with the strain. He mustn't be beaten by a blob! A wazzock like Gruey mustn't triumph over a "cool dude" like himself! What's more he stood to lose a fiver! The veins on his forehead bulged! His fingernails dug into the palms of his hands. Inch by inch he pulled back Wooly's lead.

Quidsy was screaming encouragement. "He's catching you! Come on the Masked Avenger! Keep going!"

The race was in its closing stages. Wooly was slowing down, but he was still ahead. Nidgey had made his challenge and now he had no more to give.

Gruey was in ecstasy. "He's winning! He's winning!"

A lot of punters were looking very sick. They were saying goodbye to the money they'd bet with Gruey.

Betty Woolsmith was still transfixed by the Masked Avenger's knees. "They're very knobbly. They look like . . ." Betty was blasted by the awesome truth. "They look like Peter's!"

There was no stopping her. Quidsy and Gruey tried to grab her arms but she was stronger than both of them. She ran across the finishing line directly in front of the Masked Avenger, who came to a dead stop while Nidgey ran on past and broke the tape.

Cheers from the relieved Nidgey supporters filled the waste ground as they charged forward to congratulate him. Betty was giving her son a good talking to. Wooly had stopped being the Masked Avenger and had become Peter Woolsmith with a glazed look on his face. Quidsy was shouting "Obstruction", and demanding a re-run, but nobody was interested. Mrs Grucock and Mrs Rahim had rounded on Gruey and were demanding explanations. Gruey wasn't giving any. He was more concerned about one or two of the "heavier" punters who had placed some rather large bets earlier in the day. Nidgey was with them, and now he'd got his breath back he seemed to have blood or money on his mind. Gruey knew that he had only a little money but a fair amount of blood.

He ran for it!

As he ran he could hear shouts from behind, but he kept going, only turning to look back when he thought it was safe to do so.

But it wasn't safe. Nidgey was running after him. The thought of Gruey running off with his rightful winnings had given him a second wind.

Gruey gulped and turned to race on, but he'd made a fatal error. The Wall was in front of him.

If he were to try and run round it, he'd slow down and get caught for sure. There was only one way out.

Putting on an extra spurt he charged the remaining twenty yards and leapt into space. There was a magic moment in mid-air when he knew that he was going to make it, and then an even better moment when he landed on the other side and realised that he had!

He turned to see Nidgey trying to scramble over, but he didn't care. He didn't care about anything. He'd jumped the Wall!

He swung around a lamppost while Nidgey looked at him amazed.

"I did it! I did it!" shouted Gruey. "I jumped the Wall!"

Gruey danced a dance of triumph, waving his arms like a footballer who has just scored.

As he threw his arms up and out, his wrist, still wearing his father's watch, smashed against the lamppost.

Fragments of very expensive micromachinery flew into the air and glinted in the sunshine. Gruey let out a sound that came from the very depths of his being.

"Aaaaaaaaaaaaagh!"

CHAPTER FOUR

It was a sweltering late summer day – the kind that nobody believes in any more! The terrible trio had just finished a game of cricket on the waste ground, and were having a hot irritable argument over whether Belly Before Wicket was in the rules or not.

Wooly was umpire. He was overdressed as usual, and now he was trying to make a decision while melting away under the added weight of Gruey's and Quidsy's jumpers.

"I dunno!" said Wooly, as he'd said nineteen times already. ". . . And I don't care! And it's too hot! Match abandoned! Let's go and get some ice lollies!"

The idea was a good one, but one thing was missing. Cash! Gruey's pocket money had been docked until the year 2050 to pay for his dad's watch and he now had so little that a bar of chocolate and a couple of penny bubblegums had cleaned him out. There was only one possibility.

"Quidsy . . . dy'think yer mam'll let us have one from the shop?"

It had been tried before, but Quidsy thought it was worth a try again. They set off to walk round, and then Gruey had another idea.

"You take me bike. I'm going the quick way – over the Wall."

"You gonna jump it?" said Wooly.

Gruey nodded.

Quidsy shook her head. "You won't make it!"

43

Gruey knew different. "I did last time, didn't I? I sailed it! Supergruey!"

Quidsy knew double different. "That was with Slaphead Nidgey chasin' you. It were the pressure on you made you do it."

Gruey's brain ticked and whirred. "All right! You be Nidgey, Wooly!"

Quidsy got the idea. "An' I'll be yer dad after you!"

Wooly sneered and narrowed his eyes. "Where's my tenner, you waz?"

Quidsy deepened her voice and shook her fist. "Where's my watch?"

They were very convincing. Gruey was quite shocked. "Here! Don't get carried away!"

But his friends were enjoying themselves. "Come on!" shouted Quidsy. "Let's get him!"

In an instant Gruey decided to go for it. He ran for the wall with Quidsy and Wooly after him. When he reached it he uttered a bloodcurdling karate scream and took off nose first, in a style something like a "Cumberland Roll".

Something like doesn't mean *exactly* like, and "nose first" is a dangerous angle to approach any solid object at speed.

It was a slightly changed Gruey that put his head round the door of the Rahims' shop.

"Hello," he said, in a voice that suggested he had a very bad cold. He hadn't, but his nose was certainly bigger than normal and had acquired the colour of an over-ripe tomato.

"Out!" shouted Mrs Rahim. She knew Gruey's voice. It always sounded like trouble, and she'd had enough already. Grandma Rahim was coming to visit, a very particular woman who certainly wouldn't approve of her granddaughter associating with the likes of Gruey. "Out!"

Gruey's face was replaced by Quidsy's. "Do you think we could have an ice lolly? Just a cheap one."

Wooly's joined hers round the edge of the door. "I think I might have heatstroke!"

Mr Rahim joined in, from behind the shelves where he was labelling cans. "We've no ices left! We're waiting for a delivery!"

Gruey reappeared and began a duel of wits. "How about a cold drink then?"

"Out! Go home and get a drink of water!"

"Wooly's allergic to water!"

"O.U.T. spells out."

"I haven't come in yet."

"Never mind the court case. Out!"

Gruey was just about to give in, when Mrs Rahim realised there was something different about him. "What's the matter with your nose? Some shopkeeper bang a door on it?"

"I hit it on a wall. I would've cleared it, but I weren't under enough pressure."

"*I'm* the one that's under pressure around here!"

"I'll help."

The prospect of Gruey helping made Mr Rahim pick up the labeller he'd been using and wave it defensively. "No! Don't help! Not that!"

Mrs Rahim walked over to the door and looked Gruey in the eyes, which you could still just see either side of his swelling nose.

"Most useful thing you can do is keep this shop

Gruey-free for next forty-eight hours . . . An' I want a word wi' you, Quidsia."

"What for?" said Gruey, as Quidsy was pulled in and he and Wooly were pushed out.

The door closed. He didn't get a reply.

Over in the cafe Gruey took off his left battered boot and fished a twenty pence coin out of his sock.

"It's me special hidden reserve," he said. "I pretend I haven't got it so I won't spend it, and if I get robbed they won't find it."

Wooly fanned away the cheesey pong. "Not unless they want to gas themselves! What are you gonna do with it?"

"Put it in the machine."

"Yer mad! We could get an ice lolly with it."

Gruey stuffed the coin in the machine. "There's none to buy, is there? It's typical. You get one hot spell and all the ices are sold out."

"Except dead expensive ones," said Wooly, sadly.

As usual, the Evil Commander's Spacebattle-blasters made minced microchips of Gruey's star-ships – only this time he had a really good excuse.

"Me nose gets in the way!"

"What's up with you?" asked Betty. She noticed what was fast becoming one of the wonders of the modern world in the middle of Gruey's face. "Been stickin' it where it's not wanted?"

Gruey didn't have time to tell Betty what he thought of her hysterical sense of humour. The cafe door burst open and in ran a flustered Quidsy. "Gruey! Yer bike!"

It was still there; by the wall because Betty didn't like it by the window. It was still there, but Nidgey was sitting on it, casually licking a very expensive ice lolly. "What's all the panic about? I'm just having a rest."

He looked at Gruey's swollen nose and smiled happily. Perhaps there was justice in the world after all! "Who's hit you on the snout? It weren't me, ref!"

Quidsy folded her arms and glared at him. "Get off his bike, Nidgey!"

Nidgey didn't move. "I were thinking of taking it in place of that money I'm owed from the race."

"Get off it!" said Gruey.

"Don't get in a twist!" said Nidgey, feeling a bit outnumbered. "I might want to buy it, and you need a bit of cash, don't you? I hear you're so hard up you can't afford a pair of shoes."

Gruey realised he hadn't put his boot back on from fishing out his last twenty pence. He wondered if Nidgey was at all serious.

"How much?"

"Two quid."

"Yer what?!"

"It's falling apart . . . Look!" Nidgey twanged the loose mudguard.

Gruey wasn't happy. "Oi!"

"Two fifty then! An' a lick of me ice lolly!"

Gruey was sick of the sneering tone of Nidgey's voice. He hadn't really wanted to buy the bike; more likely he'd been trying to nick it when Quidsy had spotted him.

"Get lost, Nidgey!" he shouted, and elbowed him off the saddle.

Nidgey turned and shoved the bike back at

Gruey. "Don't push me around, you dipstick! I wouldn't have yer grotty bike if you paid me!"

With that, he kicked the poor old boneshaker for good measure, flicked his lolly stick into the air and swaggered off.

Gruey leaned the bike in its more usual spot against the window, and went back inside to put on his boot. The sight of Nidgey sucking on the millionaire-type ice lolly with ice cream inside and nuts and bits on the outside had made him feel even more miserable.

"If he'd offered me a fiver for me bike I'd have taken it! I'm fed up wi' being skint all the time!"

"Why don't you hold another jumble sale," said Wooly, "like that one you did at your house?"

Quidsy remembered it. "Yeah. It were great! An' yer mam spent the whole day after going round the rest of the kids' houses, looking for her knives an' forks, an' her hairdryer, an' yer dad's electric razor, an' when she got hold of you . . ."

Gruey didn't want to hear any more. "I were only little then! Why d'y'have to be so picky? I just want some money."

Wooly suggested robbing a bank, but he didn't mean it, and luckily they were interrupted by Betty before Gruey could consider it, or who knows what might have happened. She appeared from behind the counter, looked at the scrap iron on wheels leaning against her window, and just said two words . . . quite loudly. "Gruey! Bike!"

"All right!" said Gruey. "We're going!"

As they mooched along the road Quidsy applied herself to Gruey's financial problem. "Why not do it the easy way? Just go an' ask yer dad for some pocket money."

Gruey's dad was trying to mend the portable radio on the kitchen table when Gruey tried "the easy way".

"Daaad."

"Never mind 'Dad' in that tone of voice. Whatever it is, the answer's *no*. Yer in big trouble!"

"I were just thinking about me pocket money."

"Well keep thinking, 'cos that's the nearest you'll get to any. Yer still paying for me watch you smashed – and then I find this radio in two dozen bits on the table!"

"I were fixing it."

"There were nowt wrong with it!"

"I thought there might be a loose wire."

"There certainly is a loose wire, but it's not in this radio! It's in your head!"

Mr Grucock banged the radio on the table in exasperation. To his shock it started working. Out came the dying strains of another pop classic of the sixties, and then an announcement. "Remember this is 'Youth in Action' week. Every day our radio car will be out and about looking for young people with ideas, initiative and enterprise! Young people who've put their talents to work for others in the community!"

Mr Grucock looked at his son and laughed unkindly. The voice continued. "Local firms are offering cash prizes to deserving youngsters, so ring this number if . . ."

"Don't even think about it!" said Gruey's dad as he switched it off. "They're after kids who help people, not turn their lives into a nightmare!"

His mam arrived with his tea and saw the mess that was Gruey's nose. "Stephen! You been fighting?"

"No! I banged it!"

"Come on! We'll put a proper dressing on it. It's all swollen. It looks like it might be going septic!"

His dad looked up from his slimline low fat sausages. "I expect he's been sticking it in where it's not wanted!"

Later, as he lay in bed, his nose weighed down with his mam's enormous lint and plaster, Gruey pondered on adults' sense of humour. "It can't be just coincidence. There must be some grown-up comic book they read, with all the same jokes in it!" But try as he might he could find no satisfying explanation for their daft utterances.

He switched off his thinking tackle, and turned on a dream.

A Gruey dream was normally of epic proportions in three or four dimensions, but that night it took the form of a small-scale seedy quiz show. "And now, come on down for the Youth in Action Game!" Gruey was dragged from the audience by a spangle-frocked assistant with Betty Woolsmith's face, and found he was in a studio full of television cameras, all pointing at his nose. It didn't surprise him to see that the compere in his dream was his dad.

"And now the lad with a nose for business! What's your special enterprise, Stephen Grucock? Jumping walls? Fixing radios?"

Hysterical canned laughter! Gruey felt his mouth open and speak for him. "Nightmares! I give people nightmares!"

His dad turned into a giggling wobbling jelly-baby. "Ha ha ha. I don't think we'll be giving *you* the prize, Stephen. We wouldn't *dream* of it!"

More canned laughter! As the cameras closed in on Gruey's nose, it started to swell and grow. He turned to run away, and his nose swept the front row off their seats. The laughter turned to screams. The screams turned into birdsong.

His mother turned round from opening the curtains to find Gruey sitting bolt upright in bed. "It's all right. It's morning!"

"I'm a nightmare!"

"No. You were *having* a nightmare!"

Gruey checked that his nose was big but not megalithic. He jumped out of bed, buzzing with good intentions. "I'm gonna be good today. I'm gonna have ideas . . . an' initiative, an' enterprise, an' that! An' I'm gonna earn some money!"

His mam was horrified. "Couldn't you just be quiet?"

"I wanna be helpful."

"Oh no . . ."

"I'll tidy me room!"

"What? . . . What did you say?"

"I mean it."

Mrs Grucock didn't know what to make of it. "I'll get yer breakfast," she said, and went off downstairs.

"He has me baffled," said Mr Grucock as they spooned away at their cardboard-flavoured Honey and Fibre Breksnak.

"What?" said Mrs G. "Cleaning up his room?"

"No. Why does he have to eat his breakfast off the floor, like a dog?"

"I'm reading the paper!" Gruey was on his hands and knees by the fridge, studying the newspaper laid out on the floor.

"It's last week's!" said his mam. "I put it down 'cos the floor's wet where I've been defrosting!"

Mr Grucock was in a witty frame of mind again. "Stay there if you like! We'll buy you a collar, and enrol you in the kennel club!"

"I've got it!" said Gruey.

"What? Rabies?" said his dad.

"No. It's this article about the 'Youth in Action' business. There's a kid here been doing sponsored car washes."

"So?"

"I could do yours!"

"Oh no!"

"Go on. I'm trying to be useful. Fifty pence, an' if it weren't perfect you wouldn't have to pay me!"

"Yer dead right I wouldn't!"

"It'd keep me quiet, an' out of mischief!"

Gruey's mam and dad exchanged a hopeful glance behind his back, and then gave him the conditional go ahead. "I'm coming out to inspect it afterwards," said Mr Grucock, "and it better *had* be perfect!"

It was another impossibly hot day. The sunshine bounced off the bonnet of the yellow Datsun as Gruey paused to admire his handiwork. It was beautiful. It was the work of the Mark 2 disaster-free Gruey *now with added initiative*!

He looked at his reflection in a glimmering hub-cap. It was a pity that the Mark 2 Gruey had this horrible great piece of yellow lint plastered right across its swollen snout.

As Gruey reflected on his reflection he noticed that another face had joined his. It was Wooly, formerly the Masked Avenger and now happy to be a blob again.

"Wassup? Yer dad make yer?"

"He said he'd give me fifty pence if it were perfect. Are you going down the cafe?"

"Yeah. You coming?"

"When me dad's done his inspection."

Gruey looked towards the house and noticed Quidsy standing at the other side of the car. She'd been examining the driver's door. As she left she called over her shoulder. "I should clean off that blip before yer dad sees it."

"What blip?" thought Gruey, and walked round to where Quidsy had been standing.

There was a small smudge of a mark near the handle. Gruey frowned, and gave it a rub with his polishing cloth. It was still there! It was a kind of blistery, scabby bit. It was enough to be not quite perfect, and a possible fifty pence loser.

He scratched at it with his finger nail, but it wouldn't budge. Without thinking he put his hand in his pocket, pulled out the back door key and dug at it with the door-opening end.

Too late he realised what he'd done. He'd scratched it! He'd made it worse! He looked in his cleaning kit and found a sort of washing-up scourer. Perhaps he could sort of blend it in.

No. It was worse still. It wasn't just a blip any more. It was a roughened scratched scar – in reality about two inches by two inches, and in Gruey's mind bigger than the Grand Canyon.

He cursed and ran frantically round the back of

the house, returning with a box of assorted car sprays. He fumbled quickly through them, found the yellow one, shook it and squirted it on the abominable blip.

It didn't come out in a fine mist. It came out in a grobbly dribble.

AND IT WASN'T YELLOW!

It was red. It had the wrong cap! He grabbed the red-capped one and squirted that.

It was yellow . . . but the wrong yellow. Mingled with the dribbled red, it made a nice muddy orange – if you like that sort of thing.

All sense and reason left Gruey's mind as he tried one spray after another . . . and then he heard the front door open . . .

Quickly, he kicked the box under the car, and stood in front of the terrible multicolour mess he had just so artistically created.

Mr Grucock marched down the path and stood facing Gruey. "It has to be perfect. That's what we agreed."

Gruey swallowed, and found a little voice. "Yes, dad . . . Perfect."

Slowly Mr Grucock walked round the car until he arrived back where Gruey was standing. Gruey hadn't moved one inch. His dad nodded in approval. "Not bad. Not bad at all."

Gruey chewed his lip. "It's not . . . entirely perfect . . ."

"It's good enough for me. You've done a good job there. Praise where it's due! . . . and you don't have it due very often."

"No . . ."

"Here's yer 50p, and 10p bonus for a job well done." Mr Grucock passed over the money.

Gruey put it in his pocket and breathed deeply. "I don't deserve it!"

Then, not daring to look behind him, he walked over to where his bike was propped against the railings and cycled off. His dad watched him go with something like fatherly affection. "Perhaps I've been too hard on the lad."

Absent-mindedly he turned to enjoy the sight of the sun sparkling on his beautiful shiny motor.

"Greaugheeeeeeeeeeee!"

CHAPTER FIVE

The person who answered to that cross between a name and the cry of a dying hippo flew down the street on his bike as though the devil himself were after him.

If it *had* been the devil, Gruey might have been in less trouble.

He skidded to a halt by the cafe, just as Quidsy was leaving. "I've gotta go and help me mam now!" she said. "You've been ages. Did you get yer fifty pence?"

"Oh yeah," said Gruey, "I got sixty with bonus. An' I'm gonna need it 'cos I'll have to leave home! You an' yer blip!"

"Did you fix it?"

"Yeah! Like when you pick a spot and it spreads."

Quidsy suddenly realised what must have happened. "Oh . . . Seeya later." She smiled weakly and whizzed over to the shop.

Gruey peered into the cafe. When he saw that Betty wasn't there, he propped open the door, biked straight through it, cycled up to the counter and plonked down his fifty pence.

"Give us some change Wooly, an' we'll have a game of pool."

Wooly left the money where it was. "We haven't got any change. Me mam's gone to get some. And she'll go spare if she comes back an' finds you in here wi' that, an' she'll blame me an' all!"

"Enterprise an' initiative. I'm expanding the

business. Drive-in cafe now, innit? She won't let me lean it against the winder, an' I've gotta keep an eye on it in case Nidgey nicks it or lets me tyres down."

"Yer fixated on him. Don't let him bug yer!"

"He don't bug me. I bug him. He's always after me!"

While Gruey was spouting on, the person he was spouting on about was exercising his special ability to sneak into the cafe and catch Gruey unawares.

Gruey was warming to his theme. "It's like that detective thing on the telly: *The hunter and the hunted in the jungle of the city streets.* I can scent him a mile off!" Gruey tried to sniff the air with his damaged nose.

Nidgey took a sudden grip of Gruey's shoulder. "I think yer extra-scentory powers are on the blink, superboy!"

Gruey twisted free, and turned to face his arch enemy. His arch enemy burst out laughing. "It's growing. It's gonna swell up, an' some alien's gonna burst out!"

Gruey was getting sick of nose jokes. "Give over, Nidgey!"

Nidgey rang the bell on Gruey's bike and made tutting noises about its presence in the cafe. "You'll get done when Betty gets back."

"Leave me alone!"

Nidgey put on a hurt look and a smarmy voice. "Don't fret! I were listening to you talking all that drivel and I were really upset. I'm not yer enemy. I've forgotten about all that race stuff now. It's you that starts all the trouble. I just want to be mates."

Gruey knew he was being wound up, but he couldn't help being shocked. "Mates?!"

"Yeah," said Nidgey. "This your fifty pence?"

Before Gruey could react, Nidgey had snatched Gruey's hard-earned fifty pence off the counter and was walking away with it.

"Yes! It is!" shouted Gruey, a little late.

Nidgey turned round and smirked nastily at Gruey. "I'm just borrowing it! That's what friends are for. I'll give it back later. See yer, mate!"

And then the fates, who'd been watching this scene with relish, took a hand in the turn of events.

Mr Slater, a regular cafe customer since his retirement, and an old friend of Betty Woolsmith's, was just on his way in for a late breakfast as Nidgey was making a getaway with Gruey's "borrowed" fifty pence.

It was unfortunate that, as Nidgey finished smirking nastily and turned to leave, the cafe door opened and smacked him right on the nose.

"Sorry lad," said the worried Mr Slater.

Nidgey couldn't say anything without losing face, or bursting into tears or both, so he ran off at top speed with his hand over his injury.

Gruey thought it was the best fifty pence worth of entertainment he'd ever had.

He propped himself up against his bike and shoved his bonus money in the machine. He had to waggle his head from side to side to keep his lint and plaster out of the way of the Alien Spacebattlecruisers. The problem was it made him dizzy. The other slight problem was that Mr Slater was just edging behind the bike with his tea and Betty was coming back with the change.

It was all set up. The fates gave a little push, and away it all went like a line of dominoes.

First Gruey tottering back with dizziness, then the bike falling, then the bike hitting Mr Slater on his tea-carrying arm just as Betty walked right in the path of the flying cuppa.

The fates laughed themselves sick and missed what followed. Perhaps it was too gruesome even for their taste.

Gruey sat behind the wall on the waste ground. It was one of those rare moments when he looked defeated.

Wooly arrived, leant beside him, and put in a claim for a share of the misery. "I dunno what *you've* got to complain about. I've been in the dock for half an hour, an' everything I've done wrong for the past ten years has been taken into consideration."

Gruey looked up but didn't smile. "What were the verdict?"

"Usual. I've been led astray – suspended sentence! You're banned from the cafe! And yer dad's out looking for you!"

"I know. Why d'y'think I'm hiding here? I'm bored. I'm skint again! I'm hot! I been wantin' an ice lolly since yesterday! I'm banned from the cafe! I'm banned from the shop! I've got this thing on me nose! Nidgey says I'm his mate! Me dad said I was a dog this morning! . . . I might as well be a dog!"

Wooly suddenly bobbed down behind the wall, and held his mouth to stop himself laughing. "It's Nidgey! Take a look!"

Gruey peeped over the top and saw a sight to ease his suffering heart. There was Nidgey, slumping along, with a lint and plaster on his nose, just exactly the same as Gruey's. The fates had dealt fairly after all.

Wooly and Gruey crouched down again, trying not to make too much noise. Gruey's enthusiasm for life, enterprise and initiative was completely restored. "I'll show 'em! I'll show 'em some initiative. Coal's made out of wood, y'know!"

Wooly looked at him blankly. Gruey was off again. "An' diamonds are made out of coal! Pressure . . . that's the only difference! Millions of years of pressure! Think about it! . . . Are you thinking about it, Wooly? . . ."

Wooly went home to keep out of more trouble, but the Super-pressurised Gruey Mark 3 went straight into action.

After a lot of wheedling and promising, he managed to persuade Mrs Rahim to let him help Quidsy with the shelves.

"All right, then! Take them cans off the rack, clean it up, and put them back tidy . . . I hope I don't regret this."

"You won't. I promise."

"And keep yer hands off the sweets! You can have an ice cream later, when the delivery man comes."

"Gem! Give us a cloth, Quidsy!"

With the prospect of the ice cream spurring him on, Gruey set to work. Mrs Rahim closed for lunch and made Quidsy help her in the kitchen. She thought there'd be less chance of trouble if

Quidsy and Gruey didn't work together, but she seriously underestimated the damage that Gruey could do, without any help at all.

Gruey was just starting to artistically arrange the cans and stare longingly at the sweet counter, when there was a tap at the door. Gruey went and peered round it. "We're closed."

It was Mr Slater from the cafe. He looked at the plaster on Gruey's nose and made a mistake. "Oh. It's that kid with the nose that I hit with the door. Sorry."

Gruey put him right. "No. It's the other kid with the nose that knocked you with his bike. Sorry!"

"That's all right," said Mr Slater. "I only want some shampoo."

Gruey went to get him some.

"Just a little one!" called Mr Slater. "I've not got a lot of hairs to wash."

"How about camomile to bring out the highlights in natural blonds? Will that do?"

"I expect it'll make a change!"

Just as Gruey was making this wonderful attempt at shopkeeping, the phone rang. Mr Slater looked worried. "You'd better answer the phone. I'll bring the money along later."

"Yeah, right!"

Off went Mr Slater, and Gruey picked up the fatal phone. It was the ice cream delivery service. Gruey was well pleased.

"Oh, right, yeah. Yeah! We're expecting you. Freezer's empty! Hundreds, I should think. Yeah. Them ones with the different colours ... I dunno. More than that! Yeah. Yeah. Hey, hold on, I'm not Mister ..."

But the line had gone dead and Gruey was left wondering about the possible repercussions of being mistaken for Mr Rahim.

Just then Mrs Rahim came through with Quidsy. "Was that the phone?"

Gruey shifted nervously. "Yeah. It was about the ice cream delivery. It's on its way now!"

"Good. I'm going to be busy in the kitchen. Let him in when he arrives, and put the ices in the freezer. And you can have one each. One, mind you!"

Mrs Rahim left Quidsy to help, and Gruey put thoughts of disaster out of his mind as they carried on piling up the tins and fantasised about the ice cream they'd been waiting for, for nearly two days.

"What kind are you gonna have?" said Quidsy.

"I dunno," said Gruey happily. "I want to think a bit!"

"I like choc ices best."

"Nah. They go too quick. And you have to lick the last bit out of the wrapper, 'cos it's all melted."

Quidsy thought about it. "Yeah. And the chocolate bits come off."

Gruey stacked another tin precariously high. "I like cones 'cos you can bite the ends off and suck the ice cream through."

"Yeah. The ones you get from the ice cream van are best."

"By the time I've squeezed money out of me mam an' dad, it's usually halfway round the block!"

Gruey put another tin on the pile, but a sudden bang on the door stopped them making a world record of it. Quidsy rushed to the door amidst the rolling tins. Gruey scurried round collecting them, hoping that Mrs Rahim hadn't heard, and Terry the ice cream delivery man stood there with a load of ices. A very big load of ices.

"Do you want these now, or shall I come back when you've finished playing skittles? Heh, heh. What's up with you, son? Been sticking yer nose in where it's not wanted? Is yer dad in?"

"Me mam's in but she's busy," said Quidsy. "She says you're to leave 'em, an' we'll put 'em in the freezer."

Terry pulled out a clipboard and a pen. "You must have a giant freezer! Yer dad's put in quite an order. Sign here."

Quidsy was puzzled but she signed automatically, and Terry nipped out smartish to get the rest.

Quidsy turned to Gruey. "What did he mean by that?"

Gruey looked guilty. "Maybe he thought I was yer dad on the phone."

"What did you say?"

"I just said, er, that you were a bit short of ices . . . I were using me initiative!"

Quidsy turned to look at the great stack of boxes that Terry was dumping by the door. He must have had an idea that something was wrong, but he didn't want to start sorting it out. Before Quidsy could recover from the shock, he was gone. When she found her voice she turned on Gruey. "Me mam'll go spare. They won't even fit in our little freezer, an' I've signed for 'em, an' we'll have to pay for 'em. You've done it now. We're gonna get killed."

Gruey stared at the boxes. The pressure was on.

"We gotta be quick! Some'll go in the fridge. We'd better hide the rest before yer mam sees 'em."

"They'll start melting!"

"They'll be all right for a bit. They're straight out of the deep freeze. I'll wrap 'em up in loads of paper, an' get 'em over to the den by the Wall. Wooly'll help. You come over when you get yer jobs finished!"

Quidsy didn't like the sound of it. It sounded like a Gruey disaster-movie in the making.

"We'll end up in worse trouble!"

"No we won't!" said Gruey, and then, just as Quidsy had feared, "I've gotta plan!"

CHAPTER SIX

After lunch Gruey sat in the shed with Wooly, and the newspaper-insulated boxes of rocket-boosters, jubbly-juicers and choc-o-nut specials.

He'd just finished explaining his brilliant plan. "We're gonna sell them, an' give the profits to the shop. Then they won't be so upset with me! . . . Ideas. Initiative. Enterprise!"

Wooly looked at him for a moment, and then gave his verdict. "Yer completely bonkers, you!"

If Gruey was bonkers, then Wooly must have been as well, because shortly afterwards he was helping to push the loaded-up clapped-out Grueymobile round the outside of the King Street Uptown Highprice Cinema.

The matinee queue for Superman 7 stretched round the block as usual. Nobody was sure why they didn't let people in straight away, but the kids reckoned it was either to make the film seem more popular by creating a crowd outside, or because the cinema manager was a pain in the neck who liked to make them wait.

Whatever the reason, it was an ideal business opportunity. Out of the bags on the bike came the assorted ices, and into his spiel went Gruonelli, the famous ice cream impresario.

"Come on. Getta yer ice-a-creama. Getta yer ice-a-lollies! Cheaper than inside. Getta yer ice-a-creama-here."

The kids in the queue couldn't believe their luck. They couldn't find their money fast enough. Wooly cashed it in while Gruey passed out the cold ices like hot cakes.

"Here, give us one of them toffee ones!"

"Got any banana cocktail flavour?"

"Don't you do drinks?"

Business was booming. Wooly was starting to enjoy himself. It was a Gruey plan that actually worked! But . . .

The "but" was that it worked too well. The cheerful sounds of the happy ice-lickers soon filtered through to the flappy ears of the cinema manager. His fat nose bobbed around the "Q Here" sign and his cash register eyes took in the loss to his profit.

This wasn't the free enterprise he approved of! With a wave of his fleshy forefinger, he called over the cinema commissionaire, better known to the regular customers as Mad Max. "Do you think you could sort out these lads, Mr Maxwell?"

In Mad Max's head this translated as "Go for 'em, Rover!"

Gruey was handing over a Monstrous Munchice when he felt the pavement vibrate to the rhythm of Maxwell's concrete-crunching ex-army Blakoes. He didn't need to look. He knew exactly what was coming.

"Come on Wooly! Let's get out of here!"

"Why?"

"Go!"

"But we're doing all right! . . . erk . . ." Wooly nearly fainted with terror as he saw Mad Max in full battle cry, five yards away and closing.

Minutes later everything was back to normal.

The competition had been eradicated, Mad Max was back in his cage and the usual boneheads were trying to climb in through the lavatory windows.

When they'd stopped running and got their breath back, Wooly and Gruey tried to shift the rest of their stock.

They sold three in the precinct and then discovered that nice Mr Twirly of "Buy your ice from Twisty Twirl, a treat for every boy and girl" was the sort of nasty piece of work who might slice their skulls off and scoop out their brains if they didn't move off sharpish.

They did better at the over-sixties tea dance, but the elderly ladies never seemed to sit down. After the Blue Danube, and the Anniversary, and the Vienna, Gruey decided to waltz off somewhere closer to home.

Since he had looked upon the disaster that had once been his car door, Mr Grucock had been possessed by the spirit of a reptile: Tyrannosaurus rex to be precise! He'd been out all day on a pre-histrionic rampage, looking for another smaller reptile he wanted to make extinct.

Betty was just bringing Mr Slater his after-dinner coffee when Mr Grucock-Godzilla appeared in the cafe door.

"Betty, have you seen that dogbrain son of mine in here?"

"No. He's banned at present, an' Peter's done a runner as well. I expect they're lurking in one of their usual places."

"Lurking's the right word, and when I find him

I'm gonna tear the little lurker limb from limb!"

The door shuddered as the terror of the swamps left to try elsewhere. As soon as he was gone, a little face appeared from under Mr Slater's table with an ice cream in one hand. "Here's yer sweet, Mr Slater."

When Gruey and Wooly finally made it back to base, Quidsy was waiting for them, and she wasn't happy. "Where have you been? It's taken me ages to get out. And I've got to be back again before me gran arrives tonight . . . Where are they? I'm gonna have to tell me mam, you know."

"You can't!" said Gruey. "Not yet. We've sold half of 'em, but we've still got a load of ice lollies. Wooly's been keeping 'em in his mam's fridge."

Wooly sighed. "Brilliant, innit? Yesterday we were dying for one, an' now we don't know what to do with 'em."

Gruey did. "We do! Enterprise and initiative. I saw it in the paper this morning – this kid who did a sponsored car wash."

"You tried that!" exclaimed Wooly, "and look where it's got you. On the run from yer dad!"

But it was no good trying common sense on Gruey. Once again his brainwheels were on re-spin. "No. You don't understand. Go and get Nidgey. Tell him his 'mate' wants to see him – urgent!"

Nidgey was hating Gruey on a full-time basis, but came along in the hope that he'd be able to refuse to help him out of some trouble. Perhaps he wanted his fifty pence back. Well the waz could whistle for it!

When Nidgey found out what Gruey had in mind it was a bit of a surprise. The two deadly enemies sat opposite each other and talked without arguing for over five minutes.

This was strange enough, but there was added amusement for Wooly and Quidsy. Gruey and Nidgey were facing each other like two china ducks on a mantelpiece, wearing beautifully matching lint and plaster dressings on their noses.

Quidsy couldn't resist winding them up. "Mebbee they'll catch on. Nose plasters in different colours. Could be the start of a trend . . . the Pinocchio look!"

"Give over," said Nidgey, "I'm trying to understand my 'mate' here . . . You don't want yer fifty pence back. Is that right, Gruey?"

"Not now. Anytime'll do!"

"And you want to give me a load of free ice lollies. As many as I can eat in one go. Only it has to be this evening."

"In the park. Just give us time to run round quick, and get some sponsors."

Nidgey still didn't understand. "What's it in aid of then?"

"It's a sponsored lolly lick, in aid of er . . . children in trouble."

Nidgey was strongly tempted by this charitable excuse to eat free ices, but he was still suspicious. "Where did you get the ice lollies from? Quidsy's shop?"

Quidsy butted in quickly. "Sort of."

Nidgey let it pass, but there was something else. "Why don't you lick 'em yerselves?"

Quidsy twizzled her pigtails. "We've gone right off 'em," she said, without having to lie.

"All right, but just watch it!" said Slaphead Nidgey Jackson, throwing himself into the meanest, heaviest attitude he could manage with half a first aid box on his nose. "And if there's any daft Gruey business in this . . . !"

Nidgey was lost for words. He was also lost for words later in the afternoon as the sponsored ice lolly lick got started, and the daft Gruey business began as well.

Close by the slides and the swings, with the local rentacrowd growing around him, stood Gruey, on a piece of adventure playground.

Gruey was speechmaking. Quidsy was guarding the lollies and collecting the money. Wooly was standing on a bench nearby, looking silly again, and holding a large piece of wallpaper scrolled down to the ground. The words "SPONSORED ICE LOLLY LICK. WORLD RECORD BID" were written on it in felt pen.

More kids, and a few drippy adults stopped to listen to the wonderful opportunity they were being offered by the noisy kid with the plaster on his nose and his trousers at half mast.

"Gather round ladies and gentlemen, this is your chance to sponsor Nigel Jackson in his world record breaking ice lolly licking marathon. And as a special treat for sponsors, they get the ices that Nidgey can't manage!"

This last offer caused a sudden rush of money from kids who realised they might get quite an expensive ice lolly for quite a small contribution. Quidsy looked a bit worried. Nigel Jackson was looking sick as a parrot.

"Can we get on with it! You didn't say there was gonna be all this messing about!"

"Just a few more sponsors," said Gruey, "and off you go."

Nidgey put his fist under Gruey's chin. "We start now!"

"Wassup? Are you gettin' scared?"

Nidgey nearly made contact with Gruey's chin, but he thought better of it, and shrugged carelessly. "Nowt to be scared about, is there? I'm gonna eat a load of free ice lollies, an' I'm gonna get on the radio!"

Gruey was taken by surprise. "What?! What d'y'mean 'on the radio'!?"

"Don't get over-excited! I phoned up and sponsored meself on this 'Youth in Action' thing, didn't I? There's a cash prize. I read it in the paper!"

Mr and Mrs Grucock had waited long enough. They were going to eat without him. His dad banged the radio, and out came the Grimethorpe Brass Band.

It sounded like a funeral march. Mr Grucock knew whose. "He'll show up sooner or later. And when he does . . ."

"You don't think he's run away from home or owt, do you?"

"No such luck! D'y'know what hurts me? I paid him! I paid him for wrecking me car!"

"And he was trying so hard today!"

"Terrifying innit? Him an' his flamin' initiative! D'y'think the R.S.P.C.A. would mind if we kept him chained up in the yard? We could throw him bones and take him out for walks at the weekend."

The Grucocks weren't the only people listening to Sousa's march. Mr Rahim, driving back to town with Grandma Rahim, had found himself stuck in the usual ringroad traffic jam. He reached forward and clicked the radio on. Anything would do to shut out his mother's deafening impatience.

When the band had finished, there was an announcement. "It's Youth in Action Week, so over to Jenny Stevenson, who's out and about in the radio car . . ."

Sounds of laughing and cheering, a buzz of electrical interference, and then an enthusiastic but quizzical voice. "This has to be the most unusual event of the week. Here in the park, among the swings and roundabouts, Nigel Jackson is attempting a Marathon Ice Lolly Lick."

It was a name Mr Rahim knew well. He leaned forward and concentrated as Jenny continued. "I think Nigel's lips are too frozen to talk at the moment. Quidsia Rahim – where did you get all these ice lollies?"

Mr Rahim's face turned to stone. His mother leaned forward to listen as her granddaughter's voice wavered on the air waves.

Quidsy didn't want to say exactly where she'd got the lollies. "Er . . . well . . ."

Nidgey wasn't shy. "They're from her shop. Her mam an' dad have gotta corner shop!"

Mr Rahim's face cracked into a thousand worried lines. His mother coughed with displeasure. Jenny Stevenson chirped on regardless. "Thanks, Nigel. You're not as frostbitten as I thought. Stephen Grucock, our information is that you've organised this to help children in trouble. Who are these children exactly?"

The name of Stephen Grucock was enough to explain everything. The sound of a car hooting from behind was thankfully loud enough to drown the words that came to Mr Rahim's lips as he slammed into gear, put his foot down and sent his mother flying backwards into her seat.

Back in the Grucock kitchen, Mr Grucock's fork was midway to his mouth when he heard his son start to speak. "Well . . . *we're* in trouble. Me mostly. I'm always more or less in trouble. I try using me initiative, but I have a hard time of it – with me dad especially. He's got blood pressure!"

A splutter from Mr Grucock.

"An' both me parents are a bit sykerlogical."

A gasp from Mrs Grucock.

"Me dad thought I was a dog this morning!"

Mr Grucock dropped his fork, pushed his plate aside and ran like Batman for his car.

The interview was over. Jenny was winding up her mike lead. The crowd of kids were looking unhappy, and Nidgey was looking *very* unhappy. He followed the reporter to the radio car. "Didn't we win a prize then?"

Jenny Stevenson was surprised at the cheek of it. "No. You certainly didn't! The idea was for young people to help others, not help themselves out of trouble they'd caused in the first place."

Lots of people in the crowd seemed to agree. There were cries of "Cheats!" and "What about our free ices!" Then they surged forward and started helping themselves to the remaining lollies despite all that Quidsy and Wooly could do to stop them.

Nidgey pushed through the crowd towards Gruey. His plans to make a few fast bucks from "Youth in Action" had come to nothing, and he'd been made to sound a fool on the radio. He found Gruey, and then took a grasp of Gruey's shirt collar, and shouted into his face. "You got me into this! I warned you about making a fool of me!"

Gruey pushed him off and shouted back. "I didn't tell you to phone the radio, did I? That was your stupid idea. You made a fool of yourself. You didn't need me to do it! Anyway, it weren't Radio One, were it? I bet no one were listening!"

As Gruey spoke these words, two cars screeched into the playground from different directions, and pulled up together. One of them had an unamused elderly lady in the back.

Two car doors slammed at the same time. One of them was the colour of a painter's mixing stick.

Two figures turned towards them with identical angry looks on their faces. Nidgey and Gruey looked back with identical plasters on their noses.

Quidsy made a wish that she'd never see another ice lolly in her life. Wooly wondered if his mam was on her way as well.

Nidgey looked at Gruey. "You reckon no one were listening, do yer?"

Gruey swallowed hard. "Well . . . I could be wrong about that!"

CHAPTER SEVEN

Nigel Jackson found out that a lot more people listened to local radio than he'd ever imagined. For weeks and weeks his life was plagued with, "Hiya Nidgey! How's yer numb tongue?" "Give us a fiver for children in trouble!" "Won any prizes lately, Nidgey?"

Every snide remark reminded Nidgey who was responsible for making him look a fool. As far as Nidgey was concerned Gruey hadn't suffered enough.

Gruey himself felt he had suffered a very reasonable amount. He'd had to face the wrath of his father, and the Rahims, and Betty, when she found out who'd been selling ices in the cafe.

His pocket money was back down to zero as well, but this time he learned to live with it. Business enterprises were too dangerous!

Instead he spent a lot more time at home, mucking about in the back garden, and "inventing" things that could be useful to humanity, such as stone-lobbing and welly-whanging machines.

It was probably Gruey's new outdoor garden pursuits that helped decide the next-door neighbours to move, but what finally made their minds up was when Gruey invited Wooly and Quidsy for a camp-out in his back garden.

The next morning, after a night of noise and chaos, Mr and Mrs Brett were seen queuing outside the estate agents. A few weeks later, Gruey's mam and dad were waving them goodbye.

Mr Grucock laughed bitterly. "Look! It's a white handkerchief they're waving! It's final surrender! He's won! Even if it were Mr and Mrs Rambo, he'd have driven 'em out!"

His wife knew who he meant but asked anyway. "Our Stephen, y'mean?"

"Aye. The thing from beyond that calls us mam and dad! Why can't *we* move away?"

"Don't exaggerate! He's not a bad lad!"

"No. *Sometimes* he's a little angel! *Sometimes* . . . he's asleep!"

And so he seemed to be. Upstairs in his bed, twisted up in his dream-tangled sheets, he looked like the sleeping angel described by his father.

He hadn't turned into an angel. He wasn't asleep either. He was waiting and listening. He was totally broke most of the time but there was one very important item every week which he didn't have to buy. It came with the papers, and it went on his dad's bill.

As he lay in bed with all his senses alert, he heard the expected faint creaking of the front gate. Gruey opened one eye. It might be the milkman, but he could hear no chink of bottles.

The letterbox flapped open. That narrowed it down. It might be the postman, but no, next came the rasping sound of newspaper being pushed through by some tired young person who didn't care much if it tore or not. Then the thud on the floor.

"Saturday!" yelled Gruey, opening both his eyes. "Saturday is *Timewarp!*"

With that battle cry he hurled himself out of bed, stuffed his bare feet into his shoes and banged down the stairs at breakneck speed.

Mr Grucock was savouring his buttered toast. Gruey's mam had just come in with the *Daily Dirt* when Gruey snatched the paper out of her hand, unfolded it, shook it . . . ran to the front door . . . ran back . . . and had a crisis in the kitchen.

"Where is it? It's not here! Where's me *Timewarp*? They've dunnit again! They haven't sent me *Timewarp*!"

His mam did a few of the deep breaths she'd learnt once at relaxation classes. "Don't go on, Stephen! It's a comic. It's not the end of the world!"

"Right! *End of The World*'s a *different* comic!" grumbled the unhappy Gruey. "That comes out on Wednesdays. *Timewarp* comes out on Fridays, and they deliver it Saturdays!"

"It's a wonder they don't beam it into yer bedroom," quipped his dad, as he slipped another slice into the toaster.

Gruey sat and sulked. "They're supposed to beam it through the letterbox!"

"Not any more!" said his dad.

His mam shook her head. "*Timewarp*'s been shut down. Yer father's stopped it!" She gave this information in a way that suggested that she didn't agree with this cut in normal services.

His dad felt the need to justify himself. "I don't see why he should rot his mind on my paper bill. He's warped enough as it is!"

Gruey realised he'd have to think fast. It was a case for Gruey the star defence lawyer. He went for a tried and tested opening gambit. "I bet *you* used to read comics!"

"Yeah! He did!" said his mam, now clearly a witness for the defence. *Weird Tales from the House of Horrors!* That was the stuff you read as a kid!"

The tables had been turned. Mr Grucock came back on the attack. "That were like Noddy and Big Ears compared with what he's been reading!"

Gruey Q.C. was quick to realise the implication. "How d'*you* know?"

His mam was on the ball as well. "You haven't been reading his *Timewarp*, have you?"

His dad was trapped. "Just once! Just once to see what it were about! Mad Mutant Monsters it were, from the World of the Living Dead! Worse than them videos! And it cost more than me paper!"

Mr Grucock had laid himself wide open to attack. His wife picked up the *Daily Dirt*. "That's because his comic's got more in it than your rubbish paper!"

"Don't you take his side! From now on he buys his *Timewarps* himself or he does without!"

It looked as though the prosecution were having the last word. Mr Grucock buttered himself yet another celebratory slice of toast – and then came the surprise exhibit. Gruey's mam reached under the table and pulled out a cardboard box. "Never mind, Stephen. The Bretts moved out this morning and they've left you this."

There was a note attached: "Dear Stephen, we wouldn't want your new neighbours to have an advantage we didn't, so here's all the ammunition we've collected off you over the past years!"

Mr Grucock gave a cry of horror. Gruey dived into the box and started pulling things out. "Here's me old football, an' me arrers an' me aeroplane, an' me exploding rocket, an' me ultrasonic outerspace raygun!"

Gruey pressed a button and the outerspace raygun let out a wail like fifty scalded cats. His dad grabbed the box. "That's enough! You could start a world war wi' that lot and there's new neighbours movin' in an' all!"

Gruey grabbed them back. "They're mine!"

"I'm buyin' 'em off you! Here's 50p!"

"Is that all? – What about me comic?"

There was a hushed silence in the kitchen courtroom. It was all over and the defence had won after all.

"All right! Put it back on order! I'd rather pay for you to keep yer nose in that, than cough up damages to next door on their first day!"

"Brilliant!" Gruey took the money, threw on his old blue anorak and gave a cry of victory: "Saturday is *Timewarp*!"

Then he ran out into the street, completely unaware that he'd forgotten to change into his trousers, and that his pyjama bottoms were sticking out from beneath his nylon coat in all their striped cotton glory.

As Gruey walked out of the newsagents with his *Timewarp* grasped in his hands before him, the world as we know it dissolved.

Gruey rematerialised on the far side of Sirius where Soovara, the President of the Intergalactic Congress, was waving her claws angrily inside a bubble of pure methane gas as she addressed the Head of her Security Force.

"Are you telling me, Popsquiff, that you were about to evaporate an entire solar system? And you didn't think it needed my permission?"

Popsquiff squeaked and wriggled his tentacles. Meanwhile, back in the world as we know it, Gruey's earthly body had come to a halt behind a group of people waiting to cross the road. While it stood there Gruey's timewarped mind listened to Popsquiff's explanation.

"It's just a matter of pest control. I refer to the dominant species on the third planet from the sun. If they don't destroy each other first, they could be a threat to the whole galaxy!"

The green man bleeped. The crowd crossed the road. Soovara put Popsquiff in his place.

"Silence Popsquiff! Rule 331c! Every intelligent being gets one last chance!"

A kind old lady helped Gruey's zombified body over the crossing before the lights changed. She got no thanks from the walking comic book, but she was a reading addict herself and knew the score.

Soovara gave her orders. *"Send one of your agents at once. We must try talking to these . . ."*

"Human beings, President!"

"Whatever they call themselves! We must give them a chance to reform before we evaporate them!"

This turn of events sent the Gruey mind hurtling back to his body. He looked around him at the busy street. What if it were all evaporated?

Absorbed with these cosmic questions, he never bothered to ask himself how he'd got to the other side of the road. He just pointed himself in the direction of the cafe and buried his head back in his *Timewarp*.

Popsquiff had sent the agent, but the agent was having trouble. *"This is agent Quisqaark reporting to Popsquiff. I've entered the earth's atmosphere and I'm*

*preparing for touchdown. Wait! There's something show-
ing on my vidiscreen! Missiles! I'm being attacked!
Mayday! Mayday! I'm ejecting! Aaaagh!!"*

Gruey was nearly "aaaghed" himself, but a
street sweeper took him by the shoulders and
guided him round the lamppost that was about to
attack him. By now, in the *Timewarp* world, the
destruction of Quisqaark had been noticed by a
father and son somewhere in the Midwest of
America, who'd been observing the night sky.

"Did you see that, pa?"

"Shooting star, son!"

*"No pa! It was too bright! Something flew out of it
before it exploded!"*

*"Don't talk nonsense, son! You jist git out an' feed
them chickens afore suppertime!"*

Nidgey and three of his mates, Mark, Terry, and
Mick, were hanging out by the chip shop. It wasn't
open and it wasn't about to open. But it did have a
low wall outside that was just the right height for
arm-wrestling.

Terry and Mick were locked into a no-win
competition with plenty of groan and snarl when
Nidgey noticed a comic-struck Gruey, his *Timewarp* in his hands and his head in the clouds! It
was too good a chance to miss.

"Hey! Watch this!" Nidgey walked over to
Gruey followed by Mark and Terry and Mick who
were glad to have an excuse to stop straining.
Nidgey timed his pace to a slow crawl beside the
slowly moving Gruey.

"Hello Gruey, you dozy wazzock!"

"Hello." Gruey's mouth had worked without his

81

brain, which was totally unaware of Nidgey's presence.

Nidgey tried again. "Don't you think you've gotta face like the back end of a camel?"

"Yeah," said Gruey's mouth, and the lads burst into laughter. Nidgey explained how it was done. "You can say owt to him when he's reading his comic. He's only got one brain cell and it's all used up!"

"At least he can read with it!" said Mark pointedly, looking at Nidgey.

Nidgey didn't like the implication. "Wassat supposed to mean? Come here! I'll break yer arm off!"

Forgetting Gruey, Nidgey put his arm on the wall for a wrestle. Mark parked his elbow and gripped Nidgey's hand. Just as they were about to waste a lot of energy, Mark unclasped his hand again. "Hold on! Did you notice summat funny about his trousers?"

"What do you mean?" said Nidgey.

Mark turned and stared in the direction Gruey had drifted away. "He weren't wearing any!"

Quidsy was helping her dad to fix a display of Germdeath Liquid Cleaner in the window of the shop, when she saw the blank-eyed wandering Gruey heading for the cafe. She stopped and grabbed her cardigan. "I've got to go now!"

Her dad was curious. "What's the rush?"

"There's gonna be an accident if I don't get there first."

"Where?"

"Cafe door!" said Quidsy as she dashed out.

Mrs Rahim had been listening to this exchange. She called over to her husband. "Hey, do you think she's psychic?"

"No," said Mr Rahim, looking out of the window, "I can see the accident myself."

"Where?"

"Over the road with a comic in its hand!"

The Midwest American son had done as his dad said. He was out feeding his chickens, trying to ignore the strange glow and hum in the air.

"Here you are, hens! Come and get your nice corn! Hey! What's that strange creature in the chickenshed? It looks like a giant octopus!"

In the midst of crisis in the comic world, Gruey was heading for another painful real life crisis. He was walking towards the closed cafe door at a pace that increased with the excitement of the story. In six point two five seconds he would make contact with the glass panel.

The octopus thing spoke to the all-American boy. *"Don't be afraid, earth child! I am Quisqaark, agent of Sirius. I'm badly hurt. I'm going to die! . . ."*

So was Gruey. He was about to walk into toughened glass at high speed, but just at the last moment his guardian angel Quidsy Rahim pushed the door open and he passed through unscathed.

With his attention still focused on the unlucky Quisqaark, Gruey walked through the cafe and up to the counter where Wooly was sipping an orange juice.

Quisqaark summoned all his Sirian strength to speak to the earthling. *"I've got something important to tell you. A message for all human beings . . ."*

"What are you doing out without yer trousers on?" said Wooly.

The shock of this remark pulled Gruey's mind back from the tenth dimension of *Timewarp* to the everyday world where he'd gone out in his pyjamas.

"Eh? . . . Oh no!"

"Do you know where you are?" said Quidsy.

"He's in Outer Space!" said Wooly. "He goes there every week!" Wooly took the *Timewarp* from Gruey and flicked through the pages. "What's this, then? 'Parasites from Alpha Centauri'. What do they do?"

"They take over people's bodies!"

Quidsy whispered in Wooly's ear. "They've got Gruey!"

"How can you tell?" whispered Wooly back.

Quidsy looked at Gruey's state of semi-dress.

"Stary eyes, stripy pyjamas, an' knobbly knees!"

Gruey was embarassed. "Give o'er! I was in a hurry!"

Betty Woolsmith looked up from where she was doing three breakfasts with beans. "You're a liability as it is without all this space rubbish. You want to wake your ideas up!"

Gruey didn't like all the nagging. He took his comic back and sat with it on his own at an empty table. Quidsy and Wooly went over and stood behind him.

"We're getting worried about you!" said Wooly.

"Yeah," said Quidsy. "How were you gonna get through the door if I hadn't opened it? Warp power?"

Gruey pretended to ignore her. Quidsy continued. "You take that comic too serious! I don't know what's got into you!"

"Parasites!" said Wooly. Gruey stopped pretending to read his comic and turned to the attack.

"What about Wooly, then? He's had that dice-throwing book for two years. One where you have to defeat monsters an' that! He's always at it an' he's never got past first dungeon!"

"He's not lucky with dice!" said Quidsy. "He don't get as wrapped up in that as you get in your daft comic."

Gruey's cheeks reddened. "You can't talk, anyway. What about you and them daft stickers you used to get? All that pop star rubbish! Right waste of money!"

"No it weren't!"

"Well neither's this!" said Gruey. "It's all stuff that could happen! One day maybe we'll travel to the stars, an' make contact wi' beings from other planets!"

While Gruey was making the kind of speech you get in ancient American video films, Nidgey had beamed into the cafe with his three mates in tow.

Gruey burbled on. "Perhaps one day extraterrestrial alien creatures will come and visit earth! Perhaps they've been here already!"

"I'd say they were definitely here already!" said Nidgey loudly, and pointing at Gruey at the same time. He turned to his mates in mock horror and called, "Look out, the Pyjama People have landed!"

Gruey didn't feel like putting up with any more. "Drop dead, Nidgey!"

Nidgey carried on the act for his mates' benefit.

"Go on! Zap me with yer raygun, Captain Pyjama!"

"You're way behind the times!" said Quidsy. "What are you after?"

"Nowt! We just came in to have a laugh! You any good at arm-wrestling, Captain Pyjama?"

"Galaxy Champion!" said Gruey sarcastically.

Nidgey turned serious. His plan was working out just perfectly. "Well I've just beaten these three, and here's 50p says I'll beat you!"

Money was a sore point with Gruey. "I haven't got 50p . . . unless that's the one you owe me!"

Gruey made a snatch for the money but Nidgey's hand snaked out and removed it from the table. "All right!" he said. "Let's do it for a dare!"

Nidgey looked meaningfully at the squeezy bottle of tomato ketchup on the cafe table. He picked it up and gently pressed it so that a blob of yucky red splodge appeared at the end of its dispenser.

Everybody realised what the forfeit for the loser would be. Quidsy didn't think a lot of the idea. "Betty'll go mad!"

Nidgey ignored her. He pushed in opposite Gruey and put his arm out on the table, ready for the contest. "Chicken?"

Gruey was trapped.

Five minutes later the cafe door flew open and Nidgey and Co. jostled out together. Quidsy had been right about Betty. You could hear her voice shrieking after them. "Out! Out! I don't care! I don't want to know! Dares or no dares, you're all responsible, and you're all out!"

Next out were Quidsy and Wooly. They were making all sorts of excuses, but Betty wasn't having any. "Never mind the buts! You're out!" She turned back into the cafe. "You too!"

Out came a terrible accident called Gruey, completely covered in horrible sticky red tomato ketchup, his *Timewarp* clutched still in his hand, the blobs of foul sauce splattered on his face, hands, anorak, pyjamas and shoes. You would never have thought there was so much of it in one of those little round plastic bottles.

Having thrown out all the offenders, Betty suddenly realised something. "Peter! Who said you could go, Peter? You live here!"

Wooly was hoisted inside. Nidgey went off laughing down the street. He was in the best mood he'd been in since Gruey had banged his nose.

Gruey the glob stood stickily on the pavement beside Quidsy.

"I told you!" she said.

Gruey wiped a hand through his hair and flicked a red splodge in the road. "I'm always gettin' told! I'm going home to finish me *Timewarp*."

Quidsy couldn't help feeling sorry for him. You couldn't say that Gruey deserved everything that he got. He'd only been wanting to read his comic after all. "I'll see you later," she said kindly. "I'll come round wi' Wooly when he's had his ears bent!"

"Yeah," said Gruey half-heartedly, and then laughed like the Gruey she knew. "Me mam always said I had a lotta sauce!"

CHAPTER EIGHT

While Gruey sloped off home, the new neighbours were moving in. The removal van was parked outside, and Ernie and Doreen Tresswell were supervising the shifting of a rolled-up carpet.

"Just drop it anywhere," said Doreen. "We'll sort it out when we know where we are!"

The moving men, who looked as though *they* were ready to drop anywhere, dropped the carpet in the middle of the hallway. Doreen didn't notice. She was squinting at the sky outside.

"You were so right, Ernie. I can feel the vibrations already. I can sense a presence, a watchfulness! . . . Can't you?"

Ernie Tresswell looked towards the Grucocks' house, where the blinds were twitching. "Yes, Doreen. I certainly can!"

Behind the twitching blinds Gruey's mam and dad settled back and weighed up the prospects.

"That's the last of the furniture!" said Mrs Grucock.

"Aye, and what do we know?" said Mr Grucock with disappointment. "Whole point of watching new neighbours' gear arrive is to find out about 'em! Lots of floor cushions an' you know they're trendies, lots of leather and you know they've brass, lots of high tech an' speakers an' you know you'll have to bang on the wall to shut 'em up!"

88

"There were none of that! It were all very ordinary!"

"Right! Too ordinary! They're trying to hide summat!"

"Gerraway! Yer as daft as our Stephen!"

"You what! It's your side he favours! It were *your* Uncle Bob tried to row the Channel in a bathtub!"

Mrs Grucock, busy ignoring him, looked out of the window and saw that the removal van had gone and a blue anoraked figure was trekking down the road. "Here comes Stephen now!"

As he came closer the stripes on his legs came into view. "Hey, did you realise he went out in his pyjamas! What on earth are the neighbours gonna think?"

"They'll think he's Wee Willy Winkie," said Mr Grucock, "and they could be right!"

Gruey's mam started to laugh, but by this time her son had reached the front gate and she could see that not all was well. "Oh no! He's been hurt! Stephen!!!"

She ran to the door in panic, flung it open, and there stood Gruey, comic held open, red sauce up to his timewarped eyes! She started a scream of horror, but halfway out it turned into astonishment, and by the end it was pure annoyance.

Gruey lifted his head out of the comic. "Wassup?"

Before he knew where he was Gruey had been hijacked indoors, the hot water had been run and his mam was taking revenge on his face with a rough flannel. He pulled his head out of the sink to protest. "Maaaam! I'm too old to have me head washed!"

Mrs Grucock shoved him back under the tap. "Shut up! You gave us fright of our lives!"

"It were a dare! I didn't mean . . ." His protests turned into gurgles as his mam accidentally pushed him under the water.

His dad looked across from where he was reading Gruey's *Timewarp*. "Dares! I'll give you ruddy dares in a minute!"

Ernie and Doreen Tresswell, who were watching this scene from the open doorway, now made loud coughs to announce their presence.

Doreen took a few hesitant steps. "May we come in?"

"You have done," said Mr Grucock, who had taken an instant loathing to the pair of them.

Doreen ignored the tone of his voice and continued sweetly. "The door was open. I hope you don't mind."

Ernie gave a smug smile. "We saw you watching us through the window."

"It's only natural," added Doreen, as though she meant "natural for noseyparkers".

Mrs G. tried to be friendly. "Yes, we all like to know what's going on. Our old neighbours said you were in the communication business, Mr Tresswell."

"In a way. British Telecom Accounts department!"

Doreen laughed and took her husband's arm. "I think she might have been referring to your hobby, dear."

Ernie pursed his lips. "I don't have a hobby, Doreen! I have an *interest*! Interplanetary Communications!"

"Unidentified Flying Objects," explained Doreen.

Gruey suddenly burst into life. "Flying Saucers! Yer into flying saucers?"

"Oh no!" said his dad without bothering to say it quietly.

Ernie wanted Gruey to get it right. "U.F.O.s we call them!" and then to Mr Grucock in a sneering tone, "Most informed people agree that there has to be something in them!"

"Little green men, I believe!" said Gruey's dad, sarcastically.

His mam decided it was time to say goodbye. "We're pleased you called in," said Mrs Grucock. "If there's anything we can do, you know . . . cup of sugar . . ."

". . . packet of diolythium crystals for yer warp drive!" suggested Mr Grucock with contempt.

His dad showed them the door but before he could say "goodbye and let's keep ourselves to ourselves, shall we", Gruey had offered his services. "I'll come next door an' help!"

"No!" said his dad instantly.

Ernie put on one of his range of smarmy voices. "I think it's very important to be positive with young people, don't you Mrs Grucock?"

"We'd love you to help!" gushed Doreen.

Gruey's dad appeared to be thinking for a moment, and then he laughed wickedly. "Right! You want him. You've got him. I'll send him in when he's washed his sauce off and he's out of his pyjamas."

Gruey raced excitedly upstairs. The Tresswells left, slightly puzzled about the sauce.

As soon as they were out of the door Gruey's mam and dad took a deep breath and let out a sigh of relief.

"What a pair!" said his dad. "They'd get on well with yer Uncle Bob, would them two!"

His mam was more worried. "They won't do Stephen any good. He's got a mind full of that bug-eyed stuff already! What are yer lettin' him go next door for?"

"'Cos they deserve him! There's nowt they can put in his head compared to the scrambled eggs he'll make in theirs! Give him a week and they'll be puttin' up the 'For Sale' sign!"

With that prophecy Mr Grucock picked up the *Timewarp* that had been left on the table and found his place, just as Gruey dived back down the stairs and caught him at it.

"How did it finish?" he asked on his way out.

"Quisqaark got pecked to death by chickens before he could pass on the message," said his dad. "Earth got evaporated!"

"Oh right!" said Gruey, and ran off.

Mr Grucock went back to the comic. "Happens every day, doesn't it!?"

Gruey didn't emerge from the Tresswells for two hours, which was more than enough time for a tedious argument between Doreen and Ernie about why the carpet was blocking the hallway, followed by a lot of flying saucer talk, or U.F.O. talk as Ernie had to keep reminding Gruey.

"They come in many different shapes and sizes. We don't know what they really are or where they come from. They are phenomena."

"Yeah, but have you seen any flying saucers?"

Eventually Gruey got a headful of the sort of thing he was after. When Quidsy and Wooly came round to see him as promised, they found a large map of the locality pinned up in his bedroom, with a pencilled line firmly drawn from one side to the other.

When Gruey tried to explain what this line meant, he found a certain amount of resistance.

"Gerraway!" (From Quidsy)

"Bonkers!" (From Wooly)

"No. It's right!" said Gruey. "They've got books on it an' all! Look here!" Gruey drew his finger along the pencilled line. "I've marked it out. It's called a Ley Line. It's like an old track and it goes through next door, an' down the street, an' through Quidsy's shop, an' right out to the old church in the park. It's thousands of years old, is this path."

Quidsy examined the map. "Well, it's not there now, is it? There's no path where you've drawn that line. There's all stuff in the way! What's the point of these Ley Lines?"

Gruey glanced out of the window as though he could see something the others couldn't. "Flying saucers whizz up an' down 'em! That's why E.T.'s moved in – to spot 'em!"

"I bet he is one an' all!" said Wooly, picking up a pair of deely-boppers from Gruey's junk-strewn table, shoving them on his head and attempting a spaceman impersonation. "This is Ernie Tresswell reporting to base. We have made contact with the Gruey! He is a Barmpot!"

"I bet they read the same comics as Gruey!" said Quidsy.

Gruey was getting exasperated. "All I want is for you to walk along this Ley Line with me tomorrer!"

Quidsy wasn't convinced about the Ley Line. "If it goes through our shop, how come I've never seen it?"

"It's invisible!" said Gruey quickly.

"That'd explain it!"

Wooly joined in with Quidsy's sarcastic tone. "Yeah! We'll go with you, Gruey! I'll bring me 'I-Spy Book of Space Monsters'!"

"I'm not that bothered about Monsters!" said Gruey. "But Ernie says if we follow the Ley Line, it'll build up our strength with its mysterious vibrations, an' then I'll have another arm-wrestling contest wi' Nidgey for some daft dare, an' beat him, an' it'll be a lot worse than tomato sauce!"

This was a sore point with Wooly. "I got done for that! I'll get done for this as well!"

"What is there to get done for?" said Gruey. "We're just going walking!"

Wooly frowned. "We haven't agreed to, yet!"

Early next morning three pairs of deely-bopper antennae appeared above next door's hedge. Wooly's voice came from under the first pair. "I don't see what these are gonna do for us, Gruey!"

Gruey's voice from under the second. "They'll help us pick up the vibrations, like aerials!"

And Quidsy's voice under the third. "I think I'm gettin' Radio One!"

Wooly struggled through a small gap in the hedge, getting prickled to death in the process. "I'm dyin' here! Why can't we just walk round?"

"Because," said Gruey, "you've got to follow the line exact! It's a straight track!"

"There's no track here! Only thing that ever come this way is Nidgey's dog."

"How d'y know?" said Gruey.

Wooly made a noise of disgust. "'Cos it's left a message, an' I've just put me knee in it!"

As the three Ley Line followers passed through Quidsy's shop, Mr Rahim made the same noise as Wooly had.

"Pheuw!"

"It's me knee!" said Wooly. "I tried wiping it on the grass but it won't all come off."

"That'd account for it."

Quidsy felt some explanation was necessary. "We're following the Ley Line. I think it goes out the back through the yard."

"Yes. It would, wouldn't it," said her dad.

"I didn't tell you 'cos I thought it'd take too long to explain."

"Good!" said Mrs Rahim. "We had Gruey's new neighbours in earlier on, and we don't want to hear it all again."

"Seen any flying saucers?" said Wooly cheekily.

Mrs Rahim smiled back. "Not so far today."

"No," said her husband. "Spacemen tend to do their shopping on a Thursday!"

Out the back of the shop they went, and climbed over the wall despite the fact that there was a perfectly good gate. Gruey insisted that they had to follow the path *exactly*.

They walked down the alley, across the wood yard and through some poor person's house, who was more worried about the explanation that Gruey gave than the fact that three kids wearing deely-boppers insisted they had to climb through his kitchen window.

Outside the roller-rink they consulted the map again. Even Gruey hesitated. "Are you sure it goes right through the middle?"

"Yeah," said Quidsy. "Look at the map!"

From inside they could hear the music blasting away over a base line of rumbling rubber wheels, with a treble of high-pitched screams on top.

"We'll never make it," said Wooly, but Quidsy had been skating herself. There was one chance. "There's a bit of a pause when they blow the whistle, just before they start up fast again! We'll have to be quick!"

The whistle blew. In dashed the fearless three-some. A second whistle blew, followed by squeals, thuds and shrieks, followed by moans, followed by angry voices. Out limped the fearless three-some and decided to walk around the roller-rink rather than through it.

Quidsy felt a bit frayed round the edges. "I don't think it's working too well, this Ley Line business."

"Oh yes it is!" said Wooly wearily. "The power's been flowing right through me!"

"What's it like?" said Gruey.

Pain flashed across Wooly's face. "Like I've been electrocuted!"

Nevertheless they carried on walking. It had become an obsession now. They needed to reach the end of the line, just to be able to say they'd got there.

They trudged through marshy parks, and squelched through muddy ditches. They waded through water and ran from demented dogs. When they finally reached the grassy slope in front of the old church, they collapsed, exhausted.

Wooly looked ruefully at Quidsy. "That were really easy, Quidsy!"

"We're here, aren't we!" said Quidsy. She felt she'd achieved something, even if it was daft in the first place.

Gruey had forgotten about the vibrations. All he was thinking about was his stomach. "I'll die if I don't have some grub. Didn't we bring any sarnies?"

"Have one of ours," said a voice from behind them. Surprise of surprises! It was Doreen Tresswell,, and Ernie with her. Gruey took the sandwich, and nearly devoured the tiny limp thing in one mouthful before asking . . . "What are you doing here?"

"We've been following the Ley Line!" said Doreen.

Wooly sniffed. "Where's yer deely-boppers – fer pickin' up the vibrations?" he asked scornfully.

"Oh dear," exclaimed Ernie. "I think you've misunderstood. We're dealing with very subtle forces here! You don't *pick up* the vibrations. You *sense* them. You *feel* them!"

Quidsy's brains were working. "How come we didn't see you on the way?" she asked.

Doreen offered her a mini sandwich. "We came by car."

"How could you?" said Quidsy. "There's no road!"

Gruey showed them the map. "Look! I drew the line on it where you told me, an' it didn't go anywhere near any road! There's hedges and ditches, an' cricket pitches . . ."

"An' roller-rinks!" griped Wooly. "An' wild dogs . . ."

"An' shops, an' houses an' back gardens . . ." said Quidsy.

Ernie stopped their flow. "Just hold on. Just hold your horses!" He took their map from them and applied a six-inch ruler which he carried in his top pocket along with an assortment of coloured pens, probably in alphabetical order. He laid the ruler next to Gruey's line, and moved it this way and that. Then he pronounced judgement in the tone of voice maths teachers use when they discover you've got the method right but you can't add up properly. "Oh yes. I think I see what must have happened. Your pencil slipped!"

Ernie smiled with the satisfaction of Sherlock Holmes at the end of a case. The look on Quidsy and Wooly's faces was quite different.

They were still wearing that same look in the cafe the next day. "Anyone can make a mistake!" said Gruey for the twentieth time.

Quidsy wasn't bothered. "It were a laugh!"

"Glad you think so!" said Wooly. "I've still got rollerskate marks on me backside!"

Quidsy shrugged. "It were all a bit daft, weren't it? I mean, if we were on a flying saucer track one of us would have seen 'em buzzin' about. We've lived here long enough!"

Gruey didn't think that was a fair point. "We've never looked out for 'em, have we? What about that time all the lights went out, and the television went on the blink?"

Wooly raised his eyes to heaven. "That were a power cut!"

Gruey had another theory – a second-hand

98

theory. "Ernie says it were U.F.O.s did it, but the government keeps it secret in case we panic."

"Me mam panicked anyway," said Wooly. "The telly went off right in the middle of *EastEnders*!"

"'Course it'd be dangerous for aliens to reveal themselves!" said Gruey with authority. "Look what happened to Quisqaark! . . . shot at wi' missiles, an' then chickens pecked him to death!"

Quidsy was flabbergasted. "Quisqaark?"

Wooly sighed one of his world-weary sighs. "You get worse, you!"

CHAPTER NINE

Later that evening, sitting downstairs in the kitchen, Mrs Grucock came to the same conclusion as Wooly and Quidsy.

"He's gettin' worse, that's all that's happened – an' Tresswells are as daft as he is! They read the same comics, an' they believe in 'em! It's no good expecting Stephen to drive them up the pole when they *live* up the pole!"

"Give it time," said Gruey's dad. "A close encounter with our son is summat they'll never forget!"

Excited voices could be heard coming from Gruey's bedroom.

"What's the latest?" said his mam.

"Flying saucer . . ." Mr Grucock winced and said carefully, "U . . . F . . . O spotting."

A cheap old telescope pointed out of Gruey's bedroom window. Quidsy's eye was pressed to the other end of it. Gruey was fidgeting beside her. "Can you see owt?"

"Yeah. It's really weird!"

"What is it? What can you see?"

"Nidgey in his bathroom!"

Wooly, who'd been throwing rubber-tipped darts at a photograph of a well-known quiz compere, suddenly took an interest. "What's he doing?"

"Counting hairs on his chest . . . He's stopped now."

"Don't take long to count to three," said Wooly, and went back to his darts.

"He's flexing his arm-wrestling muscles in front of the mirror now," said Quidsy.

Gruey grabbed the telescope. "Give us that! We're supposed to be watching for spacecraft!"

Watching for spacecraft didn't prove that exciting. They saw a few aeroplanes circling round for room to land, and a few seagulls who appeared to be doing the same. Wooly and Quidsy threw darts at a few more quiz show comperes and then went home. Gruey stayed up half the night, just in case he missed anything.

His mam found him slumped by the window next morning. "I blame them Tresswells," she said to his dad over breakfast. "He soaks up ideas like a dry sponge, does Stephen."

"Oh aye," said Mr Grucock, hiding a *Timewarp* behind the *Daily Dirt*.

Gruey was half awake and half concentrating on a Timewarp story of his own. *Saucers over Stonehenge!* was the title. *Have they been here before?* In drawing one, the Archdruid was giving a pep talk to an unhappy-looking Celt.

"You are the chosen one, Damaz! Climb onto the stone!"

"No! I dare not go, Archdruid! I am afraid!"

"There is nothing to fear, Damaz! Soon the sun will strike the top of the stone, and the Flying Chariot will arrive. The magic of the star people will fill you with inner strength. You will become the new Sun King!"

"Good for you, Damaz!" thought Gruey. "All I get's Sunshine Cereal!" Gruey took a slurp from the bowl his mother had left by the bed. "Yeuch! Tastes like sugar-flavoured woodchip! I bet Nidgey has rusty nails for *his* breakfast. Where am I gonna get *my* inner strength?"

Exhausted by his saucer watch, Gruey lost his half grip on the half reality of the comic, and slipped into the full-blown nonsense of a Gruey dream.

Gruaz the Great Celtic Warrior waits on the Holy Monolithic Wall in the Wasteland. The instant the setting sun touches the top of the Wall, Doreen and Ernie Starperson arrive.

"We've parked our flying chariot over by the Ley Line," says Doreen. "Where is the chosen one?"

"I am Gruaz!" says Stephen Grucock, Celtic Warrior.

Ernie pulls out a clipboard. "Sign here! Give him the power, Doreen!"

Doreen points the sacred Sunshine Cereal packet at him and a powerbolt shoots from it, making Gruaz shine like a white shirt at a disco.

"I am Gruaz the Sunshine King!"

"Oh yeah!" says a familiar voice. "And I am Nidgaz of the Three Hairs!" Nidgaz, crunching provocatively on a few six-inch nails, puts out his arm to wrestle. Down below, a figure in a black cloak is throwing dice to decide the winner.

"Oh no!" shouts Gruaz. "Not Wooly! He's useless!"

But it's too late. Wooly throws double one and Nidgaz hurls Gruaz off the Wall.

"I'm falling! Heeeeeelp!" Gruey woke up with a start before he hit the bottom of the chasm. When he opened his eyes Wooly was standing over him. "Wooly!"

"What?"

"Yer useless!"

"You're the useless one! Yer mam said I was to come up and give you a shake. Are you comin' out or are you gonna read comics all day?"

Gruey scrabbled hurriedly for his clothes. His dream had inspired him. A ludicrous Gruey theory was forming in his timewarped brain. Wooly was elbowed out of the way as he made a dash for the door. "I'll see you later! I've got summat to find out!"

Gruey leaned attentively over the back garden fence. He'd just finished expounding his ideas on druids and sunsets, and magical strength that might help you win arm-wrestling contests. He'd been testing his theory on a pair of reliable experts. "I mean how did they move all them big stones around in the first place?"

"Fascinating," said Ernie, "I've always believed there was something in it. It's possible they had strange knowledge which may have since been forgotten."

This was just what Gruey wanted to hear, but there was one little problem. "There's no Stone-henges round here, are there? D'y'think I could try it out on the wall over the waste ground?"

Doreen let out an amused titter. Ernie frowned. "Don't laugh, Doreen. It's important to be posi-tive! Who are we to tell this lad that his dream of magical strength is impossible? The power of the mind is unlimited!"

"Oh yeah," said Gruey enthusiastically, "I think that an' all!"

Gruey's ideas didn't get the same response from Quidsy. She was trying to have a game of pool with Wooly in the cafe, and she didn't want to hear any more science fiction and fantasy. "Give it a rest, Gruey! We're bored with all that now!"

Gruey was persistent. "Ernie says it might be possible. He says I might be able to invoke strange powers. Ernie says the mind is unlimited!"

"Yours might be," said Wooly, "but our minds have had enough! We walked yer Ley Line that were in the wrong place, didn't we?"

Quidsy pocketed her last stripe and turned on Gruey. "Yeah, and we looked out for yer flying saucers that stayed at home!"

"An' we're not standing on no wall waiting for you to start fizzin' and poppin' wi' star-power! If you want to beat Nidgey at arm-wrestling, do some weight training!"

Gruey could see that he wasn't going to get any support and encouragement. "Right! I'll do it on me own then! My mind's unlimited!"

With that parting shot he marched off out of the cafe. As Wooly watched him go, Quidsy placed the black neatly in the centre pocket.

"Unlimited mind! He was bad enough with his *Timewarp*. Now he's got E.T. living next door, and he believes everything he says."

Quidsy put her cue back in the rack and looked thoughtfully at Wooly. "Yeah, well I think it's about time we started making him *unbelieve*!"

Wooly scratched his ear. "How we gonna do that?"

"We teach him a lesson!"

Quidsy's lesson involved a certain amount of careful preparation. She and Wooly spent some time at the waste ground building up the crumbling edge of Gruey's favourite wall. There was no shortage of loose bricks, and after they'd pressed some earth into the spaces between them they looked solid enough to fool a timewarped Gruey.

"All we've gotta do now," said Quidsy, "is turn up casual when he's goin' about his silly stuff. Can you remember what to say?"

Wooly spoke the lines he had learned. He spoke them as though he was one of the shepherds in a junior school nativity play. "Hey-Gruey! Did-you-see-that? Just-for-a-minute-it-seemed-like-you-had-a-strange-glow-around-your-body!"

Quidsy wasn't impressed. "Don't overdo it, or he won't believe you."

"Don't worry!" said Wooly. "With an unlimited mind like his he'd believe anything!"

The sun began to set over the waste ground. It was just dipping towards the wall when Gruey arrived and clambered up onto the top. He raised his arms towards the sun, and spoke to it. "O sun! . . ." Then he dropped his arms and pulled a *Timewarp* out of his pocket to check what to say next.

"Hiya!" It was Wooly, and Quidsy with him, looking up at him from the ground.

Gruey was flummoxed. "What are *you* doing here? I thought you weren't coming!"

Quidsy gave Wooly a nudge, and he stammered a few words. "Hey . . . er . . . Did you see that?"

"What?" said Gruey.

Wooly started again. "Er, that. Did you see that?"

It was clear that Wooly had forgotten his lines. Quidsy took over. "A strange glow. There was a strange glow round you!"

Gruey started to pay attention. "You reckon?"

Quidsy struck while the iron was hot. "Mebbee it's worked! Mebbee you've been given special strength. Here, come down and give us an arm-wrestle. Test it out."

Gruey climbed off the wall. Wooly went just a bit too far. "How about wrestling us both at once?"

Luckily Gruey didn't hear the silliness in Wooly's voice. He pushed against their combined strengths, and won easily.

Quidsy feigned astonishment. "That's amazing!!"

Gruey had a twinge of suspicion. "You could be havin' me on, couldn't you?"

This was just what Quidsy had planned for. "All right! Try having a go at the wall! Give it a karate kick. I'll draw a target for you to aim at."

Quidsy pulled out a stick of chalk and drew a circle on the especially prepared piece of wall. Gruey walked back a few paces and then threw himself, Ninja-style, at the target. "Yeeeeeee – ha!"

Just like at the Battle of Jericho, the wall came tumbling down. Quidsy and Wooly grinned happily. Gruey was thoroughly impressed with himself. "I did it! It works!" He looked at the still standing portion. "I bet I could jump over it now! I bet I could sail it easy!"

This was something Wooly and Quidsy hadn't bargained for. But it was too late to stop him. He skipped lightly up to the wall that he'd charged in vain a hundred times, flicked himself into the air on one leg . . . sailed over . . . and then leapt even higher with delight. "Yeah! I've got the power!"

After a brief victory dance Gruey ran off at speed. Quidsy shouted after him. "Where you goin'?"

"I'm off to get Nidgey!" he called, and disappeared down a back alley.

By the time Wooly and Quidsy caught up with him it was too late. The challenge had been made, and accepted with pleasure by Nidgey.

It was late in the evening now, and most kids had wandered off home for their teas. Even so the word got around, and a little audience gathered at the waste ground for the contest. There were two milk crates for seats, and a box between them for the wrestlers to lean on. Gruey and Nidgey were discussing the forfeit.

"What's it gonna be this time, Captain Pyjama? More sauce?"

Gruey, full of imagined sun power, looked at the muddy ditch were the J.C.B. had been at work. "Not this time, Nidgey! This time the loser gets rolled in the mud, an' covered wi' flour!"

There were cheers from the audience at the prospect of this entertainment. Gruey produced a bag of flour he'd brought with him for the purpose.

"Best of three?"

"Suits me!" said Nidgey.

Nidgey's seconds took his jacket. Wooly and Quidsy used the opportunity to whisper urgently to Gruey. "It were us," said Quidsy. "We fixed the wall. It were a trick to teach you a lesson!"

Gruey wouldn't believe her. "It can't be. I jumped it!"

"You can anyway. It's just confidence."

Nidgey was sat waiting. Gruey felt his super strength fading with the sunlight.

"Are you gonna call if off?" asked Wooly.

Gruey looked at the growing crowd of blood-thirsty spectators. "How can I?" he sighed.

From over the other side of the waste ground Ernie and Doreen Tresswell could faintly hear a crowd of people chanting "One . . . Two . . . Three . . ." but they didn't pay any attention to it. They were concentrating on something much more important.

Ernie was sitting facing the French windows with a very serious expression on his face and a priest-like tone to his voice. "Oh, beings from beyond this world – speak to us, speak to us with your minds!"

Doreen was sitting next to him with a slight lack of concentration. "I feel a bit silly, Ernie."

"You must take this seriously, Doreen. What is the point of us moving here in the first place if we don't make some effort to make contact!"

"Yes, but I'm not sure what I should be doing."

"Focus your mind. Imagine that someone out there can hear us!"

Someone could! Two floury muddy battered boots were standing just outside the French windows. The owner of the boots was feeling unhappy, and feeling that, although he'd landed himself in it, he'd been badly led astray and encouraged by a right pair of wazzocks.

The floury boots went for a little walk next door, and found the ultrasonic outerspace raygun still in the cardboard box, under the kitchen table. When they returned Ernie and Doreen had their eyes closed and their sixth and seventh senses well tuned. "I can feel something coming through, Doreen."

"What's it like?"

"Like a presence ... a vibration! There's definitely something there!"

A noise like fifty scalded cats rent the evening air. As they opened their eyes in shock, Doreen and Ernie were treated to the sight of a strange black and white dusted figure, with a ghastly white face and staring dark eyes, banging on their window.

Ernie went rigid with fear as though he would never move again. Doreen screamed and shouted so loudly that it could be heard from one end of the estate to the other. "Aaagh! Ernie! Help! It's the beings from beyond!"

Exactly one week after they moved in, the Tresswells put up the "For Sale" sign, which proved to the Grucocks that Mr Grucock was psychic. Another week later the last of the

Tresswells' furniture was loaded into the van. Gruey's dad watched through the window as the carpet went out the way it came in. He chuckled and waved. Then he turned to his son, who was reading the latest *Timewarp* on the kitchen table.

"Go on Stephen! Tell us it again!"

Stephen looked up from his comic and smiled. "The thing is, I still don't know why they were so upset about the beings from beyond. After all . . . they *were* expecting them!"

CHAPTER TEN

After the Tresswells had taken off for the planet of their choice, Gruey's mam and dad went through one of the stages parents go through sometimes, where they think that their children might not be Slug-monsters from the crypt after all. No mention was made of broken watches, resprayed cars or the price of comics for more than two weeks.

But Gruey wasn't content. He felt he needed to achieve something, something to show he could do some good for people, something to show that he still believed in himself.

Then his opportunity knocked. Despite the latest theory that nothing except computer science and spelling counted as education, Gruey's school decided to put on a drama production. The show they decided to put on was *Oliver*, and Oliver was the part that Gruey decided he was going to play.

Quidsy decided that she was going to be Nancy, and Gruey and Quidsy decided that Wooly would have to be something in it whether he liked it or not.

There was just the problem of the audition, but for someone like Gruey, who believed in himself, it posed no difficulty. It just meant that his mam and dad had to listen to a lot of "Food, glorious food" while he practised. By the morning of the audition they were beginning to get just a little tired of it.

Gruey picked up his holdall and made ready to leave. Then he stopped for assurance from his mam. "Do you think I'll get the part?"

"Mebbee. Just do yer best, and don't get yer hopes too high!"

"Yeah, but I've gotta have confidence! I've gotta believe in meself!"

Mrs Grucock felt some realism was needed. "You can have too much of a good thing! I'd sing a bit more quietly and try and get a few notes right!"

Mrs Grucock had been very kind with her last-minute advice. The problems with Gruey's voice were twofold: 1 It was very loud. 2 It was very horrible. But Gruey thought he sounded like a nightingale and just couldn't understand why the music teacher was almost in tears during the audition. He was still mulling it over as he traipsed home afterwards, with the equally disappointed Quidsy and the blissfully relieved Wooly.

Nobody spoke till they reached the cafe. Just as he arrived at the door, Gruey had a thought. "Maybe I should've sung quiet like me mam said."

"Definitely!" said Wooly.

Gruey was down but not beaten. "I still think I'd have made a great Oliver . . . and Quidsy would've made a great Nancy!"

Quidsy wasn't bothered. "I'd gone off bein' Nancy anyroad. She was a right drippy-drawers! – Always fainting, an' wailing, an' gettin' killed! She should have given that Bill Sikes a bash over the head with a frying pan!"

"Yeah, like *you* did!" said Wooly. "Why d'y'think you didn't get the part?"

"I only meant to give him a little tap!"

"Sounded like the school bell!"

"You didn't even stay to do your bit!"

"I'm not so mad keen to try an' make a fool of meself!"

"No. You do that without trying!"

Gruey was getting tired of the slanging match. "Don't start, you two!"

"I'm not startin'!" snapped Wooly. "Yer just brassed off, both of you, 'cos you fancied being stars!" Having made what he thought was a pretty stunning point Wooly walked into the cafe.

Gruey dumped his bike against the cafe window and followed after him. "It weren't fair! That's all! It weren't fair!"

Quidsy was in straight after. "No. It weren't. Maureen Nolan's playing Nancy and she's a right drip."

Betty watched them come in. It didn't take her half a second to weigh up what had happened. "I gather none of you got a part, then?"

Gruey put the money for a drink on the counter, but didn't speak. Betty continued. "No need to get upset about it. You do enough play-acting as it is! Shame though, I were looking forward to all them evening rehearsals!"

"Why's that?" said Wooly.

Betty plonked down the drinks. "'Cos you'd be *there* instead of *here!*

"Give over!" said Quidsy. "We're not so bad!"

"Not so bad as what? A herd of elephants? At least the elephants don't park their bloomin' bikes up against my window!"

Gruey started to shuffle out to move it, but Betty stopped him. "Don't bother! It's only glass, isn't it? It'll only break, won't it? What's a few more quid here or there?"

"Eh?" Gruey was shocked. This didn't sound like Betty at all. She saw the puzzlement in his face and tried to explain. "You get less worried about that sort of thing as you get older. I don't expect you kids to understand."

Gruey didn't understand. He noticed that she hadn't taken his money from the counter. He picked it up and offered it to her. "Here y'are!"

"What's this?"

"Money for drinks."

"Have them fer nowt! You're only here for a short time, aren't you?"

Quidsy was worried. As soon as they were sat at a table Quidsy asked Wooly what was up with his mam.

"It's her birthday next week," explained Wooly. "They get like that, old'uns."

Gruey wanted to know if he'd bought her a present.

"Not yet. She says she don't want no fuss made."

"She don't mean that though, does she?" said Quidsy.

"No. She means the opposite. I'll get her summat nice, and then she'll tell me how I shouldn't have, and how I'm a smashin' lad really, an' I won't get done for the next twenty-four hours!"

Gruey nodded. "Yeah! Then it'll be back to normal! My mam's the same."

"And mine," said Quidsy, but she never got to

go into detail because the cafe door swung open and there stood Nidgey, with his dog Fang on a lead, making a trumpet fanfare sound with his mouth. "Here we are, fans! Nigel Jackson Superstar . . . and Fang the Wonderdog! Who wants me autograph?"

Gruey was astonished. "You never gotta part!?"

Nidgey announced to the whole cafe that he had indeed got a part. "I'm Bill Sikes and this here's me dog, Bullseye! The other kid dropped out after Quidsy tried to brain him wi' frying pan!"

There was one rule about the cafe that Betty was going to enforce whether it was coming up to her fortieth birthday or not. "No dogs allowed! Get him out!"

Nidgey went for a snide sidestep. "You've let these three in!" he sneered looking over at Gruey, Quidsy and Wooly.

For a moment it was like Dodge City Saloon. Quidsy stood up and pushed her chair back. Wooly reached for the pepper without really thinking what he would do with it. Gruey just sat there and drawled as coolly as he could. "Watch it, Nidgey!"

Nidgey went for one of his really witty back-answers. "No! You watch it! I'm in it! You're the rejects, an' we're the stars!" Then, considering he'd won the war of words, he walked out. "Come on Fang! We don't want to hang around wi' dross!"

Quidsy couldn't believe it. "How'd that happen?"

Gruey was boiling with rage. "Fix! It must've been a fix!"

"Now, now! Don't go gettin' jealous!" said Betty, trying to calm them down.

"I'm not," said Gruey indignantly. "I believe in meself! It's just hard believing in yerself when nobody else believes in you!" He stood up and looked sadly into the distance. "I'd have been Oliver if I'd sung quieter!"

Quidsy and Wooly couldn't think of anything to say. It wasn't like Gruey to be knocked down so easily. "It's really got to him, hasn't it?" said Quidsy, after Gruey had gone off home.

"Don't worry," said Wooly. "He'll recover!"

It was easier said by Wooly than done by Gruey. Later that night Gruey sat on his bed, listening to the music blasting out on his radio. He was sitting on the bed in the dark, cross-legged, covered completely in blankets like a human wigwam. He'd gone straight upstairs without any tea and hadn't said a word to his parents all evening. He hadn't recovered!

After they thought he'd had long enough, his mam and dad came up to his room, turned on the light, turned off the radio, and attempted communication.

Mr Grucock tried first. "Come on, son. You can't sit up here sulking like this all night!" Gruey was motionless. It looked as though he could. "You in there?"

His dad wasn't getting anywhere. His mam tried. "Didn't they even offer you a little part?"

Gruey poked a nose out. "Yeah! They said I could be a workhouse boy as long as I didn't mind miming the songs instead of singing, an' I didn't mind playing the one wi' bad legs so I didn't run about!"

"Well, it were a start," said his mam gently.

Gruey stuck his head out. "What at? You wouldn't know *when* I'd started and *when* I'd stopped!"

Back he went under the blankets. His dad patted the place where he thought Gruey's head was. "I know what you mean. Only play I were ever in were 'Sleeping Beauty' and I had to be a tree! Me mam made me a great costume wi' brown tights an' a woolly green blob thing wi' a pigeon on me head but teacher said I had to take it off 'cos it were gettin' too many laughs. Then I got relegated to a bush 'cos I kept dozin' off!"

This bit of information was too much for Gruey. He started laughing and had to come out for air. His dad was pleased about that. "That's better. We're not used to seein' you like this!"

"No," said his mam. "Way you normally go on you'd have started up yer own show by now!"

Mr Grucock agreed. "Aye! We're lucky there! He'd have his mates round for rehearsals – banging on floor, an' thieving clothes out of the cupboard!"

A sudden change came over Gruey. "Thassit! Why didn't I think of it?"

"What?" said the alarmed Mr Grucock.

"What you just said! Yer brilliant! Yer the best mam an' dad I've ever had!"

"We're the only ones, aren't we?" said his mam. Gruey didn't hear her. He was too busy fantasising.

"Me own show! And you can be in the front row on first night!" His mam and dad gave each other a look that suggested they weren't sure how much of a privilege that might be.

Next morning their fears were justified. They were downstairs while the rehearsal was going on upstairs, and if the noise was anything to go by they were already in the front row. Mr Grucock slammed the door leading up to Gruey's bedroom. It didn't make a lot of difference.

A bloodcurdling scream came from above, and then the sound of a cap gun going off.

Gruey's dad shook his head. "Don't sound like any show I know." From upstairs came another scream, an evil laugh and a loud thud.

"I think it's called *Count Dracula meets the 'A' Team*!" said his mam.

Upstairs Gruey's bedroom had been transformed into a theatre studio. The curtains were drawn, and a red bulb in Gruey's bedside lamp created the right late-night movie atmosphere. Gruey, in his dad's old coat, his mum's floppy hat and a pair of sharp white plastic gnashers from the joke shop, was flapping down on Wooly, who looked a treat in Mrs Grucock's wedding dress. Just as Count Grukula was preparing for an illegal blood transfusion from Woolheima's milk-white throat, Mrs Q. of the "A" Team Vampire Squad burst out of the bedroom cupboard.

"Freeze, you bloodsucker!"

"Get lost!" said the undead one. "Bullets can't kill a vampire!"

Quidsy took off her dark glasses. "It's hopeless, is this! We should do summat with more action in it!"

Wooly had an idea for some action. "Come down the shopping centre wi' me an' help me find a present for me mam!"

"Not if yer goin' out dressed like that!" said Gruey. Wooly made an exasperated noise, and started struggling out of his frock.

"What's up wi' you, Wooly?" said Quidsy. "You've bin mitherin' all mornin'!"

Wooly finally pulled the bodice over his head and told her. "I'm bothered about me mam! . . . She's worried about summat . . . apart from gettin' old an' that! You know when it's important 'cos they don't tell you!"

Quidsy gave him a hug. "Don't worry. We'll buy her a really nice present! Whatever it is, that'll cheer her up." She touched the two ends of her pigtails together and an electric spark of an idea flashed between them. "I know! Down by the market! There's one of them bargain shops there . . . feller with a microphone! He flogs all sorts!"

He certainly did. Later that evening Wooly, Quidsy and Gruey sat in Gruey's bedroom around a cardboard box. They didn't seem overjoyed with their purchase.

"That's brilliant, that!" said Gruey. "She'll really appreciate it! Her very own F.B.I. Detective Kit!"

Quidsy picked it up and read the contents on the back. " 'Wi' cap gun . . . an' holster . . . an' a special badge!' Yer mam'll have a great time! There's handcuffs here as well! I expect she'll use 'em on Gruey!"

Gruey thought that was unfair. "It were Wooly's fault!"

"I told you!" said Wooly. "I stuck me hand up for the vase. How were I to know he'd gone on to the next item? Mebbee he'll take it back . . ."

"Fat chance!" said Gruey.

That seemed to put the full stop on it. They carried on sitting glumly, looking at the world's most unlikely present to give your mam unless she's an F.B.I. agent in which case she'll have one already.

Then Quidsy's hair started computing again. "Never mind! We'll use the kit for our show! We'll do a detective!"

Gruey was impressed. "Yer brilliant, Quidsy!"

Wooly wasn't. "But I've no prezzy fer me mam!"

Gruey explained. "We'll do the *show* for yer mam!"

"Oh yeah!" said Wooly without any enthusiasm. "She'll love that!"

But little lights were shining in Gruey's eyes and they were theatre spotlights! "She will! She'll love it! We'll make a cake, an' have a party an' all!"

Quidsy was getting carried away as well. "Yeah! It'll be like Royal Variety Night, only Betty'll be the Queen!"

"And we'll invite our mams and dads and all the kids who go in the cafe!" Gruey was seeing his dream of stardom spring back into life.

"Everyone'll be there!"

"Even Nidgey!"

As Quidsy pronounced the name of his mortal enemy, Gruey's tide of generosity turned. "No need to go *that* far!"

CHAPTER ELEVEN

Betty was very popular with parents. After all, she was practically running a youth club in the cafe, even though she swore she wasn't.

She was also a special friend of the Rahims, so when Quidsy brought Wooly and Gruey into the shop, and started reading off a birthday party shopping list they didn't turn a hair – even when Quidsy got onto the second page.

"... an' we'll need some lemonade, an' crisps an' peanuts, an' ice cream, an' stuff fer sandwiches ..."

Her dad stopped her before she could start on the third page. "Don't worry, Quidsia. We'll sort it out."

Gruey couldn't quite believe what he was hearing. "What about money?"

"You won't need any," said Mrs Rahim. "It'll be our present to Betty."

"Great! Fantastic! Yer brilliant!" burbled the jubilant Gruey, and pulled out another list. "We'll need some eggs an' some flour, an' some icing sugar, an' lemons ... for the cake! I'm gonna make a giant birthday cake!"

Mrs Rahim didn't need to think twice about the possible consequences of Gruey baking. "You'd better leave that to me!"

Gruey was abashed. "Why? I like cooking! Me domestic science report said I was very creative!"

"That's why!" said Mrs Rahim. " ... Oh, all right. We'll make it together."

Quidsy was concerned about security. "You won't tell Betty, will you mam?"

"Of course not! It's a surprise, isn't it!"

"I've told Mr Slater," said Gruey, "'cos he's her mate, and he's always in the cafe. He's gonna help us do the decorations. And me mam and dad know 'cos of rehearsals . . ."

"We're doin' a surprise show as well!" said Quidsy.

Mr Rahim looked just a little worried. "What kind of show?"

"We haven't rehearsed it yet," said Quidsy.

"It'll be exciting though!" said Gruey.

Wooly gave a wry smile. "Action-packed!"

Half an hour later rehearsals were in full swing at the Grucocks, and Gruey's mam and dad were finding out just how action-packed it was. The ceiling bounced like a trampoline as various television detectives jumped off fast-moving trains, speeding trucks, and medium high roof-tops – all played by Gruey's bed!

Mr Grucock swallowed a couple of headache pills and shouted up the stairs. "Give us a break, will you!"

Gruey's voice shouted down. "We're rehears-ing!"

"Rehearse a quiet bit, then! There must *be* one! By the time we see this show we'll have heard it fifty times through the ceiling!"

After Mr Grucock had made his point the noise stopped. Nor did it start up again in a few minutes as might be expected. There was no noise because there was no rehearsal going on.

They were having a serious difference of opinion.

Wooly was getting impatient. "Come on. We've only got till Wednesday. Make yer minds up!"

Gruey had made his mind up. "Starsky and Hutch!"

Quidsy had made hers up too. "Cagney and Lacey!"

Wooly had made his mind up that there was nothing to make his mind up about. "Who cares? They're all the same!"

"Are they heck!" said Quidsy. "There's women detectives!"

Gruey didn't want to be a woman detective. Wooly wanted them to stop arguing and get on with it. "Why can't we just have one of each?"

"Starsky and Lacey!" suggested Gruey.

"Cagney and Hutch!" said Quidsy to be different.

"What about me?" asked Wooly.

Gruey added on another detective. "There's no lack of 'em is there? How about Cagney and Hutch . . . and Dempsey!"

Quidsy thought this was going too far. "Wooly can't be a detective!"

"Why not?" asked the affronted Wooly.

"'Cos then there'll be nowt to detect, will there? There's gotta be a crime! There's gotta be somebody that gets robbed, or kidnapped . . ."

"Or tied to a lump of concrete an' lobbed in the river," shouted Gruey.

Quidsy was full of ideas. "Or wired up wi' dynamite . . . an' they've lit the fuse! Fzzzzzzzz!"

Quidsy and Gruey were now in the middle of an all-action adventure. Gruey and Hutch checked his F.B.I. computerwatch. "Do you think

123

we'll make it, Cagney?"

Quidsy crouched behind Gruey's quilt-covered cadillac. "I don't know, Hutch! We're running out of time!"

During this breathtaking life or death crisis Wooly walked over to the door. "Don't fret yerselves! Take as long as you like!"

Cagney and Hutch were left in freeze frame. Gruey gave Wooly a worried glance. "Where are you going?"

"Home!"

"Why?"

"'Cos it's gonna be me, innit? I'm the one that's gonna get kidnapped and blown up! You get the best parts an' I get to look a complete wally!"

Gruey was mortified. "Yer won't be a wally, Wooly." And then, just as he said those two words, Wally and Wooly, he noticed a similarity, and couldn't help opening his big mouth. "Hey, I never thought of that: Wally – Wooly; there's hardly any difference."

Wooly slammed the door, and stomped down the stairs.

Quidsy turned on Gruey. "Now you've done it!"

Apart from Mr Slater, Betty's cafe was empty. It was like that most of the time, and that wasn't good for business. Betty was thinking about the hard work and the little reward and her fortieth birthday coming up soon. As she weighed up the state of things, she fidgeted with a brown envelope she'd had from the estate agents a few days ago. Wooly had been right. There was something she hadn't told him.

Mr Slater tried to jog her out of her mood. "Looking forward to your birthday?"

Betty gazed at the envelope. "It'll just be a day like any other."

"You never know!" said Mr Slater, trying hard. "I'll tell you what. If all else fails, I'll take you out for a fish supper! How about that?"

"You're very kind," said Betty, "but it's not really my birthday that's bothering me."

She was just about to tell Mr Slater what was on her mind when a blob in a mood walked in.

Mr Slater carried on with his cheering-up. "Hello, Peter. Where's rest of the gang?"

Wooly ignored him and walked on past till his mother caught hold of him. "Hey! Mr Slater's speaking to you! Come here and sit down."

Peter did as he had to, but he still didn't speak.

"What's up?" asked Betty. "You've gotta face like a wet week. What is it?"

Wooly shrugged. "Nowt."

Betty looked for sympathy to Mr Slater. "Kids!" she muttered. Mr Slater nodded in agreement, and made a little sign to her that he'd try and find out what had upset her son.

When she'd gone out the back Mr Slater turned to Wooly. "Now then! Is it them two hooligans you hang about with?"

Wooly gave a grimace that might have had a bit of smile in it. In about half an hour Mr Slater had the full story and had arranged a peace conference over on the waste ground.

Gruey made profuse apologies and agreed that while Wally was a bit like Wooly, on the other hand Gruey rhymed with pooey, so what was in a name?

The casting was more of a problem. Wooly was determined not to be battered, blown up, dumped in the river with concrete overshoes or staked out in the desert sun to be eaten by camel spiders. The negotiations took some time but eventually it was sorted.

"It's a deal!" said Wooly. "As long as I don't get done in it."

"Not any more," said Quidsy. "We're doin' Cagney, Hutch and Dempsey in 'The Mafia Cafe Affair', an' I'm Cagney."

"An' I'm Hutch now," said Wooly, well pleased with the new arrangements. "I'm Hutch, an' Gruey's the lady that owns the cafe in the story."

"Only I'm really Dempsey in disguise!" added Gruey quickly. "An' I get to capture the villain in the end."

"An' it's a comedy," said Wooly.

Mr Slater didn't think there was much doubt about that, but there was still a problem, and Quidsy felt it had to be sorted.

"It's no good having all detectives if we haven't got anybody to be a crook!"

"True," said Mr Slater, "but I've been thinking . . . You haven't invited Nidgey to this do, have you?"

Gruey bristled at this possibility. "No way! Mind you, knowing him, he'll find out and turn up anyway. He'll come to make fun and cause trouble."

"There's not much doubt about that," said Mr Slater. "But what if he had a part to play? There wouldn't be much chance of him spoiling it then, would there? And he wouldn't be in the school play if he wasn't up to scratch, and he'd certainly make a good villain!"

Quidsy suddenly realised what Mr Slater was suggesting. "You don't mean . . . ?"

Gruey knew what he meant, and he knew how he felt about it. "No! No, I'm not having it! No!"

Next morning, outside the school gates, Quidsy and Wooly were still trying to talk Gruey into Mr Slater's plan. Gruey hadn't budged. "No! I don't want him in it! He's me mortal enemy. It's like asking Doctor Who to do a double act with a dalek!"

"He does!" said Wooly. "You have to have the nasties or it doesn't work!"

Quidsy was firm. "Anyway I'm director, an' I've asked Nidgey already. I said it were a difficult part, an' we couldn't do without him, an' he'd be brilliant."

Gruey groaned miserably. Quidsy continued. "An' he said he'd do it on account of how it was for Betty. There's only one condition. Gruey has to ask him nicely."

Gruey's mouth opened. "What?"

"He's waitin' over there by the wall," said Quidsy. Gruey was enraged. "I'm not crawlin' to him! You know what he's like! He'll want to start taking over!"

Wooly thought Gruey was taking his feud with Nidgey too far. They'd never get the play done at this rate. He reminded Gruey what it was all about. "It's for me mam, innit? We've only one more day!"

Gruey stopped and seemed to be considering what Wooly had said. Then he gave a malicious little grin. "All right! He's in!"

Wooly was astonished at this quick turn around, but went off to get Nidgey quick before Gruey could change his mind.

Quidsy was also curious about the quick switch. "How come?" she asked, while Wooly was getting Nidgey.

"It's for Betty," said Gruey. "It's a special occasion! . . . Plus I've just thought of summat else. You know that last scene? Well if Nidgey plays the villain, that means he has to kneel down and beg me for mercy. That's the way we wrote it! And he has to do it with everybody watching. It's a beaut!"

Quidsy was about to say something about not being so daft when Nidgey sauntered up. Gruey spoke first. "You wanna be in our show then?"

"Dunno. You askin' me to be in it?"

"I'm askin' you."

Nidgey felt he'd had his pound of flesh. He held out his hand. "Right. Seein' as it's for Betty's birthday . . . Truce!"

Gruey took the hand he'd never grasped in friendship before. "Truce."

The earth didn't shake, no choirs sang and the birds didn't fall out of the trees with shock.

Nidgey had agreed because he was now convinced that he was a star of stage and screen. His fans had the right to see him perform, and it was only natural that Gruey should be begging him to be in it. Of course Nidgey was going to steal the show, and everybody would be able to see that he was a brilliant actor, and Gruey was a wazzock!

Gruey was just thinking about the last scene. He didn't care if it was play-acting or real life. He was going to triumph at last.

Their hands were shaking but inside their heads they were still putting the boot in.

There was only that evening to rehearse Nidgey but it wasn't difficult. He really was good at acting, even though he showed off nonstop. The problem was the last scene. They never quite got round to practising it. When they stopped to go home and still hadn't done it, Gruey said, "We'll make up that bit on the night. It's dead easy. You'll get the idea."

But Nidgey didn't get the idea. "What *does* happen at the end?"

Gruey had to tell him. "There's a fight and you get beaten!"

"You what!"

"I'm Dempsey in disguise," said Gruey, "and I get you in a hammerlock, and you cry for mercy!"

"From you!"

Quidsy stepped in quickly before they lost their new performer. "It's acting, innit! Yer supposed to be a good actor."

It worked. "I am," said Nidgey modestly. "Yer lucky to have me."

"Yer not gonna let us down?" said Quidsy, as Nidgey started to leave.

Nidgey smirked with pleasure. "I'll be there! I expect there'll be a lotta people in the cafe tomorrow, what wi' me fans an' all, so just remember to speak up, an' don't forget to face the audience. Just keep an eye on me an' you'll get the idea!"

Gruey, Wooly and Quidsy just sat there, astonished.

"See you then!" said Nidgey.

As soon as he'd left Wooly erupted in indignation. "Big head!"

"I told you what would happen, didn't I?" crowed Gruey. "There's only one reason it's worth putting up with him. That last scene . . . it's a beaut!"

"There is another reason," said Wooly firmly. "It's me mam's birthday, and we want everything to go right. So don't turn it into a Nidgey–Gruey dust-up like everything else!"

"It won't be!" said Gruey, reassuringly but not convincingly. "I'm goin' over to Quidsy's to make yer mam's cake tonight . . . She don't suspect owt, does she?"

"Not a thing!" said Wooly. "She'll think we've forgotten her."

CHAPTER TWELVE

Betty thought they'd forgotten her. She took Mr Slater's card and propped it up on the counter with all the other cards she hadn't received. "Very kind of you, Mr Slater. I'll put it here with me collection."

Mr Slater managed some classy acting of his own. He gazed sadly at the lonely little birthday greeting. "Oh dear. Didn't you even get one from Peter?"

Betty put on a brave face and made a joke out of it. "I told him not to bother and he didn't. Never mind, though. Mrs Rahim took pity on me the other day. She's invited me over for a birthday cup of tea when I close."

Mr Slater had a mission to accomplish. "You go now, Betty. I'll look after things till you get back. It's not busy, is it?"

"No. It never is!" said Betty, pulling the now crumpled brown envelope out of her pocket. "And I've made me mind up about this as well."

Mr Slater didn't know what she was talking about since she'd never got round to telling him what was in it. In any case he had no time now to investigate. He had to get her out of the cafe. "Give my love to Mrs Rahim!" he said, as he ushered her towards the door. "I'll see you later! Don't forget to leave room for our fish supper!"

The Birthday Action Squad were ducked down behind the shop counter with all the gear they needed to shift over to the cafe. The Rahims were keeping lookout. Gruey was worrying. "What about the cake? Is it done?"

"Calm down!" said Mrs Rahim. "Mr Slater's got it hidden over the cafe."

"Is it enormous, though?"

"Not as enormous as it was before half the mixture went on the kitchen walls, but it's big enough!"

All eyes turned to Gruey, and he had to confess. "I got the speed wrong on the mixer, didn't I? . . . Look out! Here she comes! Out the back door an' over the cafe!"

Quidsy and Wooly started to gather their gear, with Mr Rahim shooing them on. "Don't hang about! We can't keep her here for ever!"

As Betty Woolsmith went in through the front door Stephen Grucock, Quidsia Rahim and Peter Woolsmith went out through the back. It was like escape from Colditz, ducking and diving along the street, with boxes of sandwiches and decorations balanced on Gruey's bike.

Mr Slater let them in, and they went to work. Streamers streamed across the ceiling. Balloons clustered in corners. In double quick time the tables were moved over to make a buffet, and the chairs gathered to face a makeshift stage. A banner with "Happy Birthday Betty!" stretched over the windows.

And the cake! . . . The cake was everything that Gruey hoped it would be, a monster of a many-layered chocolate glory, overburdened with icing and walled round with piped cream.

Full supporting cast included sandwiches, sausage rolls, kebabs, bajis, trifles, dips, spreads, crisps, peanuts and gallons of different fruit juices and fizzy pops. It looked like the last scene in the comic where Lord Snooty and his pals get the grub!

And they had to keep their hands off it! It was unbearable!

Betty was sitting on the Rahims' comfy sofa, about to reach for a scone, when Mrs Rahim whisked them away from her. "I'll take these away, Betty. We don't want to spoil your appetite for later!"

"What later?" said Betty. "Only offer I've had for later is a fish supper for two with Mr Slater." As she spoke her hand found the crinkled brown envelope, still in her pocket. She decided she'd have to tell someone soon, and it might as well be now. ". . . Oh yes. There is another kind of offer I've had. It's an offer for the cafe, flat as well. I've more or less decided to sell up."

The Rahims were genuinely shocked. Mr Rahim was upset that she hadn't said anything before. "Why didn't you say? You don't have to do that, Betty! If it's a loan you need . . . ?"

"That's kind of you . . ." interrupted Betty, "but it's not just the money, it's . . . well . . . it's just one day the same after another . . . Sorry, I shouldn't get morbid on me birthday, should I? I'll drink me tea and get going. I've left poor Mr Slater on his own."

Mr Slater wasn't anywhere near on his own. All

the kids from the neighbourhood were crowded into the cafe, and quite a few adults as well. There was confusion and shouting, at least two tape machines playing at once, Fang barking for the fun of it and Wooly over by the window trying to see what was happening at the shop. "The door's opening!"

Gruey peered under the banner. "She's coming!"

"Get the lights out!" shouted Quidsy. "Turn off them tapes! Quiet."

All the noise and clatter had stopped. Someone shuffled. Someone went shhhh. Even Fang stopped barking. In a few seconds, all you could hear was breathing. There was a shaft of light as the door opened, a split-second view of a slightly suspicious-looking face, and then a completely gobsmacked Betty Woolsmith as the cafe erupted into life.

"Surprise!" shouted Quidsy and Gruey. "Happy Birthday Mam!" shouted Wooly. And then everyone started singing "Happy Birthday dear Betty", as they led her down the aisles of seats to the front.

Quidsy's mam and dad had come across as well, and Gruey's parents, and Mr Slater, wearing quite a spivvy suit. Betty was completely overcome. The tears were rolling. She didn't know if she was laughing or crying. ". . . I . . . I don't know what to say. It's not exactly a fish supper is it, Mr Slater?"

Out went the lights again, and out came the cake, aglow with candles for Betty to exercise her lung power. She didn't manage it in one, but then hardly anyone ever does. She was too excited to make her breath work properly and in the end everybody helped and everybody cheered when Betty managed the last one . . . and cheered when it came alight again because Gruey had substituted one of those everlasting trick candles!

Then the cake was put on a table to one side, and Gruey, wearing the same frock of his mam's that had starred in *Dracula meets the 'A' Team* took the centre stage. "Ladies and gentlemen . . ." Whistles, cat calls, and a cry of "Is that you in there, Gruey?" from Betty. Gruey continued. "In honour of Wooly's mam, we would like to present, *The Mafia Cafe Affair*."

Mad cheers!

"Starring Cagney and Hutch!"

More mad cheers as Wooly and Quidsy jumped in from the wings with their F.B.I. guns aimed at the audience.

"Hands up!" said Quidsy, and most of the audience did as they were told.

"Cool it!" shouted Wooly, adjusting his dark glasses.

"Help! It's the Return of the Masked Avenger!" cried some clever dick.

Gruey resumed his introductions. "Starring Big Mac the Mafia Hitman!"

Nidgey shouldered onto the stage wearing the kind of jacket that gets stuck in doors. His mates went wild with enthusiasm.

Gruey introduced himself. "Starring Bessie the Cafe Lady, who isn't all she seems to be!"

"Yer not kidding! . . . Get on with it!"

The show started. Big Mac muscled in on the cafe. "O.K. Bessie . . . Dis your nice little cafe?"

"Out! Out! I'm not havin' you leaning your Alfa Romeo against my winder!"

Betty heckled happily. "Cheek! Who's that supposed to be?"

Big Mac gave it some straight talk. "Don't talk to me like dat, lady. I see you've got yerself a nice little business."

"You must be joking!" said Bessie. "There's only these daft kids ever come in here! And they've never got any money, and they're always wreckin' the machines!"

Betty was helpless with laughter. She thought it was a hoot to see herself taken off so well.

Big Mac was explaining what he meant. "I mean if you want dis place to stay nice, you better give a little donation to da big boss's insurance fund!"

Bessie wasn't easy to blackmail. "Get lost! I'm with the Prudential!"

"O.K. sister! We'll play it your way!"

With these ominous words Big Mac swaggered off, and Bessie revealed that she was really Dempsey and it was all part of a combined operation with Cagney and Hutch to put Big Mac behind bars.

Betty sat watching this nonsense in a state of continuous giggles. She was having a much better time than if she was the Queen at the Royal Variety. "I am enjoying meself, Mr Slater. After all I've been saying! Were you behind all this?"

"It were the kids organised it, Betty. They've got a soft spot for you."

"I've been thinking of selling up."

"I thought as much!"

"Isn't that cake beautiful!"

"Gruey made it . . . with some help."

"It must be the first daft thing he's done that hasn't made me want to murder him!"

Back on stage the plot had thickened. Cagney was checking out the score. "O.K. Dempsey! He really thinks you're a poor defenceless old lady."

"Less of the old!" shouted Betty.

Hutch reminded them of the plan. "As soon as he gets through the door we jump him."

"Leave him to me," said Dempsey, with a bit of Gruey showing through. "I've got scores to settle with 'Big Mac'."

Gruey/Dempsey ducked behind the counter. There was an intake of breath from the audience as they realised it wasn't all play-acting. "Watch it Nidgey!" shouted one of his mates, and Nidgey, waiting to come onstage as Big Mac, realised in one moment what it was all about. His mouth set in a grim smile as he walked on and said his lines. "O.K. I'm gonna tear this joint apart!"

Gruey's head popped up from behind the counter. "Not so fast, Mac!"

The two arch-enemies stood facing each other. The show was evaporating and real life was taking over. Nidgey was thinking about the race and the ice lolly lick. Gruey was thinking about the fifty pence he was still owed, and a lot of sauce, mud and flour.

Neither moved or spoke but there was plenty of silent understanding. The adults thought maybe they'd forgotten their lines, but one of Nidgey's mates shouted out, "Get him, Nidgey!"

For a moment Nidgey was distracted. Gruey grabbed him in a hammerlock. It looked real, but it was actually a part of the rehearsed play . . . so far!

Fang started barking from the audience. Gruey came out with his lines. "Beg for mercy, Big Mac!" He nearly said "Nidgey", but stopped himself just in time. Not that it mattered any more.

"No way!" said Nidgey, and threw Gruey off his back.

Gruey picked himself off the floor. "Hey! That's not in the show!"

There was plenty of noise from the audience now as they tried to work out if they were faking or not.

"Yer not makin' a fool out of me again!" shouted Nidgey. "It's a new ending. Big Mac escapes!"

Nidgey started to swagger off. The Nidgey fans cheered, but Gruey wasn't going to let him get away with it. "No, he doesn't escape!" he shouted, ran towards the retreating Nidgey and dived for him with a tackle that would have got him a place in Leeds R.F.C.

Unfortunately, although the tackle was a work of art the aim was less than perfect. Gruey's outstretched arms missed Nidgey altogether, and his face landed slap squelch in the middle of Betty's cake. There was a horrified silence apart from Nidgey who was laughing fit to bust a gut. Gruey wiped the cream from his eyes, picked up a trifle and shoved it squarely into Nidgey's face. Except that Nidgey moved at the last minute and it was Betty who received her sweet before her main course.

She was not amused. "It's always the same in the end, isn't it Gruey? Well here's summat I've always wanted to do." With that she gave Gruey a nice creamy cheese dip, upside down on his head. Cheers filled the cafe. Mr Grucock jumped out of his seat. "Me too! I've always wanted to do that!"

And he did!'

That was the beginning of the silliness, which only ended after Quidsy had emptied a jug of orange juice over Nidgey, and Betty had shouted very loudly and seriously, "That's it! That's enough now! Everybody out! Go on the lot of you! Out of my cafe!"

Everyone stopped and looked at Betty, and remembered it was her birthday, and looked at the mess, and felt very stupid and sorry. Gruey's face was sorriest and saddest of all. It looked like a sad clown's from the circus.

Betty smiled at it, and then roared with laughter. "All right. It's not as bad as it looks. There's plenty left to eat, and I don't mind my cake a bit squashy . . . but what were meant to happen at end of the show?"

"Villains are brought to justice!" said Wooly.

"And everybody lives happy ever after," said Quidsy. Gruey looked at Betty, and at the mess that needed cleaning up. "It doesn't happen like that in real life, does it?"

"No," said Betty, taking the brown envelope out of her pocket . . . and tearing it in two. "Not all the time."